# Tempted by the Protector

Barbara Winkes

ISBN: 978-1-7781247-6-1

Created with Atticus

*For D.*

# Chapter One

## Saoirse

Peace is a fleeting moment. It looks like I've found mine here in the Irish countryside, alone among strangers, with just enough geographical distance from past failures and regrets. I have many, and some days, it strikes me as ironic that no matter how far I go, I'm still connected to the family, my temporary home the cottage that Tommy Flynn left me in his will.

Wrong or right, that's debatable, given that this was where he spent the first romantic summer with his then bride-to-be Courtney.

Which is perhaps irrelevant on some level, because we were never more than friends, no matter how much his parents might have desired me to be their daughter-in-law. That's all gone now, anyway. There wasn't exactly bad blood between me, Rory and Ciara, but I knew they were wary.

The FBI came looking around once more. They got off relatively unscathed, and I could part ways with them on a semi-friendly basis.

The rest...It's still turmoil at times, and the soul-sucking guilt can catch me off guard, even though I know the events that unfolded weren't my fault. If anything, Tommy would be happy to know that Courtney is safe and sound. The same goes for me, I guess.

He had a local look after the place, and so, there wasn't much to do when I arrived, just turn on water and electricity, dust the surfaces, and I was home. For a while, at least.

The longer I stay here, pretending to myself that I'm looking for a buyer, the less I want to face the questions at home, about my future, my career, and the rest of my life without the Flynns in it, my best friend, and the people who had become parental figures to me.

I can't hold off those questions forever, but for the time being, I am happy to be here, read, take long hikes when the weather allows and spend a good number of my evenings at the local pub run by a woman named Keira Brady.

I'm happy to be just Saoirse, without the obligations and pressure of my former job, the expectations of loyalty and secrecy.

Some of the locals knew Tommy, as he had been in town for business a time or two, but few made the connection.

It's good to be by myself while I figure things out, far away from the family, and the nosy questions of the FBI. You'd think I'd given them, and Special Agent Farmer in particular, enough to keep them off my back for a while. She knew that there was a line I wouldn't cross.

Tommy's attorney had assured me that no one else knew about this property.

Imagine my surprise when Rory Flynn called me.

⁓⁓⁓

Even though my scenic hike was cut short today by worsening rain, I am calm, probably the most I've ever been in my life. I would have scoffed if anyone had predicted it, the idea that a place that I had never visited before could call to me like this. I enjoyed my life, my job. Protecting the people closest to me was what I did, and I was good at it.

Until...Well, that wasn't my fault, not really, and I've come as far as believing it on most days.

I open the door to Keira's pub. One of the regulars gives me a wave, and Keira, who's behind the counter, smiles at me. I find myself a table in a corner in the back, and she joins me a moment later.

"Good evening, Saoirse. What can I bring you?"

I'll admit that I had a bit of trouble with her accent the first few times. I might have the name and the looks, but I was, like my parents, born in the US.

Regardless, I've come to feel at home, in this town, and this place in particular.

I make my choice quickly. I'm not above being somewhat predictable, or clichés, if you will, but Keira's stews are legendary, and the best meal at the end of a cold, rainy day like this. A Guinness to go with it.

I'm grateful that the locals are friendly but get the message to leave me alone otherwise. I can—somewhat—belong, without the pressure I was used to back home. It's new. It's good. I might never return.

My phone rings as I'm in the middle of my meal. I almost don't hear it over the background of music and chatter, but given how few people have this number, I am tempted.

Temptation is never a good thing.

"Saoirse," Rory Flynn says. "How are you?"

He, too, is friendly. I tell myself he has no reason to act otherwise. If anything, my connection to Special Agent Farmer has kept him and his wife out of prison.

"Rory. It's been a while." I left the family before the ultimate conclusion, when it became clear that he was putting too much faith into the words of a corrupt cop and showing little consideration for his widowed daughter-in-law.

"Too long," he says, sounding ruefully. "You know we loved you like the daughter we never had."

Is he drunk? Am I? He's laying it on thick, which is ringing alarm bells for me.

"Not anymore, that is?" I ask with a wry laugh. "Should I be worried?"

"Saoirse, don't be ridiculous. You have nothing to worry about."

That is a relief, I guess. Regardless, he has already disturbed my peace. No one was supposed to know I'm here, though I'm not surprised he still has valuable connections.

"In fact," Rory continues, "I have a favor to ask. For a friend of mine."

"I don't want to be rude, but please, ask someone else. I don't work for you anymore."

"I'm aware. This would be a one-time job. No strings attached, I swear."

It sounds too easy. It's not like I couldn't use the money now that I'm apparently staying here to figure out my life.

"You did go to some lengths to find me."

"Oh, please." He almost huffs. "Like you didn't know Tommy told us he was going to leave you the cottage."

I suppose it's possible, since he also told his parents that Courtney is bi.

"What about Mr. Connelly, does he have nothing to worry about either?" I ask, half serious. Rory could still cause one hell of a lot of trouble for the attorney, if he thinks he made the wrong choices for the family. For me, too, if I'm honest.

"Are you going to help me or not?"

"I need a bit more information," I say, and finally, that feels good. When a Flynn says "jump," I don't ask "how high?" anymore.

"Aria Bellini is missing," he replies.

"She sounds musical." I take a sip of my Guiness. "Should that name ring a bell?"

"She's Antonio's daughter. He's afraid that something might have happened to her."

Oh, crap. This is bad news. I didn't think Rory would take his newfound ceasefire with his Italian counterparts this far. It's one thing to bury the feud with the Carusos. I have a lot of respect for Sienna. Aligning with Antonio Bellini is something else.

"First of all, I won't do a job for Bellini. He's not someone you want to be associated with either."

"He's a father who's scared for his daughter," Rory argues. "I can relate to that. I failed to protect my son."

"You didn't. I did."

The words are out of my mouth before I can stop myself, and I realize he's played me well, my grief, my guilt, even though I have no doubt that his match mine.

"No, Saoirse. We've been over this." When I don't say anything, he continues, "Aria was supposed to arrive in London yesterday. She didn't. Antonio's head of security claims he saw her board the plane. She never showed up at the hotel."

"You want me to go to London?"

At least he's not asking me to report to him at the mansion, that's a plus.

"You have many sources, and you're good at this, Saoirse. I think that Antonio has reason to be worried. He recently had a business deal fall through and received some threats. This might not be a coincidence."

"I'm not the police. I'm sure Bellini has some friends there, so he should call them. I'm sorry, Rory—I think it would be best for both of us to stay out of it."

"Saoirse, the man has a lot of power here at home. It would be beneficial to nurture a good relationship."

I have no idea what he has gotten himself into, and for the first time since the Flynns gave me a job and a home, I don't want to know.

Time to move on.

"I'm going to send you—"

"Bye, Rory," I say and end the call.

My stew has gotten cold, and I wave over the server and ask if they could warm it up for me. Then I ask for another beer.

—ele—

I'm still not drunk. A little tipsy maybe when I leave the pub and walk home, or whatever home is at this moment, deeply nostalgic. Rory and Ciara are, well, set in their ways, the business, the connections, the family. There was a time when all of this tradition, predictability and comfort, appealed to me, because it was so different from my own upbringing. Truth be told, at some point even the idea of being Mrs. Flynn appealed to me, but that was a short, fleeting time, long gone.

In the cottage, I light a fire in the living room fireplace—there are, in fact, multiple ones on this property. I could make this into an Airb'n'B maybe, get some income from it.

Or I could take that job.

I laugh to myself. It's ridiculous to think about. Sure, I could probably find out if Aria ever arrived in London. I might even be able to find her, but do I want to? Right now, all I want is a piece of that apple cake I bought yesterday, and perhaps a coffee with a shot of something. That sounds good. A real comfort.

My phone buzzes again as I prepare my dessert and carry it back to the coffee table. I pull my legs up under me and open the message. Fuck you, Rory. He's still trying to play me, and he's doing it well.

The first thing I see is the picture of Aria Bellini. She looks painfully young in it. Aria is twenty-seven, and word has it her father has watched her like a hawk since her mother Marina went missing when Aria was thirteen years old.

Which might be understandable, but at the same time, I remember hearing stories about the Bellini family when I was still employed with Rory and Ciara. I'm not sure what prompted his change of heart. Rory used to be careful to the point of paranoia, and the fact that he wasn't going out of his way to exploit the most vulnerable, worked for me.

Don't get me wrong, there was a lot of illegal action behind the legal business. No victimless crimes either, but as long as the right people paid...

I frown at the documents he's sent me. Bellini might have had a point. When the deal fell through, he still gained millions while the partner went out of business.

Regardless, trying to go after Aria sounds like a bad idea when she's been protected by an army of security guards until now. Bellini's people are highly trained, and the head of his private force, Victor, is said to have ties to the Russian mob.

Again, many reasons not to get involved. Rory didn't seem to be in distress, so I assume he genuinely believes in forging a good relationship with this man. Well, good luck with that. I don't want any part of it. No matter how much that picture is haunting me, the scared lost look behind the smile.

# Chapter Two

## Aria

I am free. The realization comes as a shock to me, an unfamiliar, exhilarating, and frightening feeling. For the first time in my life, I am completely on my own. I treasure this rare, impossible moment, amazed at every turn.

That Victor fell for it. That I'm on a plane to Paris instead of London, three days before my scheduled journey. I ask for wine with my meal, almost surprised when the flight attendant doesn't object. Of course, I'm not a child, I've just been treated like one my entire adult life, and for some reason, I thought I might look like one too.

Twenty-five-thousand miles up in the air, far away from home, I can admit that I played a part in it. When my mother went missing, it changed our lives irreversibly, and I assume Dad was afraid of losing me too.

I had bodyguards wherever I went, which made the weird kid stand out even more. I have always hated it, but there was a time when I could understand it. At least until he brought Victor on board, who started out as a guard and quickly became head of security. I liked the former guy, a retired cop who left me with as much privacy as possible, a grandfatherly presence in the background. Until, one day, he was gone.

As I'm having my meal, I remember asking about him. Both Dad and Victor dismissed my question.

Victor has mostly been polite with me, save for one time. I know he's loyal to Dad. Lately, I can't shake the feeling that he's hoping for more.

Dad who has been distant since Mom disappeared, has started joking about how it's time to find me a husband. At least I hope he was joking, though I can't be too sure. He's closer to Victor than he's ever been, and I'm afraid he's preparing him for the role of man of the house.

In our circles, it would never occur to a father that a daughter could take the reins, or maybe it's just my family, because I've heard about Sienna Caruso and Kendall Mancini. I've admired these women from afar, in secret, because no one in my house has a good word to say about them.

I have another secret, and for the sake of my life and happiness, I started taking precautions after Victor tried to kiss me. He apologized right afterwards, begged me not to tell Dad. Some of those pieces don't fit together, and I knew I couldn't sit and wait around for them to fall.

Victor could become a problem, but that's never been the whole story. I don't want to marry him, or any man Dad might consider appropriate.

It took me almost three months to convince Dad I could travel to London on my own, as long as I would meet with Uncle Luigi the moment I cleared customs.

When he finally, reluctantly said yes, it was a condition that Victor would stay with me until I got in line to board, which meant he had to buy a ticket as well.

I bit my tongue, determined not to start a fight, because in that case, he would have sent Victor to go with me all the way.

Fortunately, as head of security, he has things to do other than babysit me. I got away from him long enough to get into a cab to the airport, three days before my scheduled flight, while Dad was out of town.

Paris, here I come. I won't stay long. Avoiding an ill-fated marriage and an overbearing father is not the only reason for my travels, they're just the most urgent one. But there's time for everything else until I feel safe.

I didn't dare book anything online, so a few hours later, I stumble through the city jetlagged, clutching my bag tightly. First, I buy a phone. I took the SIM card out of the old one and disposed of card and phone separately at the airport.

Next, I walk into a random hotel, and fortunately for me, I can rent a room for a couple of days. It's expensive maybe, but I want to stay close to the train station, just in case.

The next steps are planned as well and in as much detail as possible. I had spent a bit of money on pre-paid credit cards, not enough to raise anyone's suspicions at home. If asked, I could say it was for gifts.

Obviously, I couldn't transport heaps of cash. I don't think I would have made it through security, so this is the next best option.

I sit in the hotel lobby with a coffee while the staff gets my room ready for me, watch people come and go, listen to their exchanges. I'm really here. I did it.

I almost nod off when close to me, a family walks by. When the toddler drops his toy, I jump, but it's nothing dangerous, no vengeful husband to-be, or angry father has followed me. Am I finally in a place where the Bellini name doesn't have so much weight?

I sure hope so.

First of all, I need to sleep.

This is only the beginning.

A few hours of sleep worked like magic. I get dressed again, since it's still early, and leave the hotel to explore the neighborhood, and have dinner and a glass of wine in a small bistro.

Back at home, my father would watch me at meals, make sure I didn't drink too much, didn't dress or act inappropriately when he had clients over.

It's unbelievable that I'm here in another country, where I can do, eat and drink whatever I want. I want it to stay that way. I'm not sure yet where I'll end up, or how I'm going to pay for my new life once the money runs out, but I'm optimistic. Delusional maybe, but who can blame me? For the first time in many years, I feel like I have a chance at forging my own destiny. I will make it count—and hopefully, solve a mystery along the way.

I never planned to stay longer in Paris, but once I've had a good night's sleep and my continental breakfast including a buttery croissant with strawberry jam, everything that came before, and what might lie in my future, is at a glorious distance. It's sunny outside and so I spend the entire day walking, take the subway to different stops, and generally revel in the beauty of the city.

There's no time to get in line at the most famous museums, but I manage to visit a couple anyway, including the *Petit Palais* which is free. I cover an admirable amount of landmarks during that day. At night, watching the illuminated Eiffel Tower at the Champs de Mars, I wish I could stay longer. Maybe next time. My future is wide open now.

The next morning, I check out early and take the train to Munich. People get on and off, and I realize that no one pays me much attention other than the occasional greeting. I can finally relax, watch the scenery fly by, read half of the book I bought at the station, and a magazine cover to cover.

When someone comes by with a refreshment cart, I buy coffee and a snack.

I nap a little, too, but jolt awake every few minutes, too worried I might miss my stop.

Finally in Munich, I find myself in another giant bustling train station. I walk around a bit and buy a pretzel for lunch.

This journey still feels strangely unreal, and at the same time, it comes with an emotion I barely recognize. I'm happy. Excited to be here, on the way to find closure and the new life I've been dreaming of since my teenage years.

You'd think Dad would miss me given that he paid his men a lot to make sure I didn't vanish like my mother, but I've long realized that he cares about appearances most of all. And I might have had illusions about reforming the business, but he would never allow it.

The marriage talk was the last straw.

It's warm and humid in Munich, and so I just hang out near the station, waiting for the time to board another train. Tomorrow at this time, I'll be in Rome, my final destination for now.

Maybe I'm fooling myself, and it wouldn't take all that long to figure out where I am, but I tried to be careful. Yes, I've asked questions that earned me raised eyebrows, but I haven't asked *those* questions in a while. Years, actually, while the desire to know the truth kept building.

I still have some time before the money runs out, maybe enough to find it. And then, I'll really be free.

Trying to save money, I booked a reclining seat rather than a cabin on the night train, my only piece of luggage stowed safely between me and the window. I had a few curious looks, from airport security and hotel staff when I arrived with only a tote bag, but since the X-ray showed nothing alarming, they bought my story.

An extra shirt, a toothbrush, socks and underwear. Up until the last moment, I harbored the fear that Victor might be rooting through my purse, but of course he expected me to leave for London days later. I can only hope that the trace is cold enough for me to do what I came to do in Rome and then slip away unnoticed.

I need new clothes. And a haircut maybe. Aria Bellini, the girl who shuts up when they tell her not to ask any more questions, is vanishing. I'm surprisingly okay with that.

My arrival in Rome feels like a déjà-vu: Another morning in an unfamiliar city, exhaustion, the necessity to find a place to stay.

I used the free wi-fi at the hotel in Paris to look up my next accommodations on the new phone, and thank God, I can go straight to my room. It's a bit noisy, but I still fall asleep right away, into jumbled dreams of an irate Victor, Dad chastising me, and a woman with red hair. I wake up disoriented, shaken, and a bit amused about the turn of that dream.

It's not like I can involve anyone else in this. It's too dangerous. I can't hope for anyone to rescue me either. This journey to myself clearly comes with challenges, but I'm in it now, and I'm never going back.

# Chapter Three

## Saoirse

Rory left me alone for months, now he has sent three text messages in as many days. The tone clearly tells me he's trying to butter me up. I haven't deleted them yet, but it's not because it's working, I tell myself. I might not even call him back.

I did, however, set things in motion to try and find out more about Aria Bellini's whereabouts.

Maybe I need a challenge more than I can admit, or maybe I'm starting to believe that something bad might happen to her if we don't find her, that I could be the one to prevent it.

That's dangerous, delusional thinking, and yet...Here we are.

It's obvious why Bellini can't and won't involve the police, which means precious time has already been lost. I call in every favor I've collected over the years (though I know better than to contact Special Agent Farmer on this) and once Aria shows up on security camera footage in Paris, I manage the rest. There are still many mysteries to this. She doesn't look to be in distress, so I assume she went freely. From Paris to Munich and then to Rome—is it a random route, or is there intent behind it? To do what? Aria will inherit one of the biggest criminal fortunes in the country. She can't possibly be running from that, can she?

I've been around the children of these families for a long time, and I know a thing or two about them. They always come home. Sometimes it takes emotional blackmail, or the reminder of what life would be like without all that money and power.

Tommy was at times deeply conflicted about his family, the business, but he stepped up when his parents needed him to. He was proud to provide this life for Courtney and his son, Oliver.

There is no mention of a partner in Aria's life. I don't doubt that she, too, is proud. Tommy's act of rebellion was to marry Courtney. Maybe this is Aria's.

The next time Rory calls me, I pick up from a small Roman café where I'm having breakfast. My language skills might not be enough to make me pass as a local, but at least I know to order my cappuccino in the morning.

"So, how is this going to work?" I ask. "Who's paying me?"

"I already did," he says, sounding relieved. "I'll send you the details for the account. Thank you, Saoirse. This means a lot."

"Wait a second. I didn't say I was going to do it."

"But you will."

"I'm thinking about it," I admit. "I think your friend is lucky, by the way. No one has harmed her."

"They still might. He says they were angry about how the deal went, and Aria was specifically mentioned in those threats."

That might even be true.

"Do you know where she is?"

"As a matter of fact, I think I do." I keep it vague for some reason I'm not yet sure about. Of course, I know where Aria is, in the hotel across the street. I plan to shadow her today, see what's on her agenda, if anyone is following her.

I might approach her, try to assess if she's in any danger, then step away.

"I knew you could do it! Keep up the great work. One more thing, Saoirse. Antonio would like for you to accompany her back home, so he knows she'll be safe all the way. You'll be reimbursed, of course."

Something feels wrong about this. Rory should still be mad at me for leaving.

"What are you up to? You know that if it wasn't for me, your entire family would be behind bars."

Maybe not the best course of action, but I'm cranky with the lack of sleep, and Rome wasn't in my planned travel itinerary.

"And I appreciate everything you've done for us," he returns. "Please. This is not about the past. It's just helping out a friend, and I know you're the best person for the job. That's what I told him."

"Okay. Aria never went to London. She came to Rome, but I don't know for what. Maybe she wants to do some sightseeing in peace."

Rory ignores the slight rebuke.

"Without telling anyone, after what happened to her mother? Aria has obligations to her family, and if you're right, she's acting irresponsibly right now. Besides, she could still be in danger. Do you have an address?"

I hesitate for a split-second. "Not yet, but I'll figure it out. I'll get back to you. About that bank account..."

"In your inbox in a few seconds. I appreciate it, and Antonio will, too."

Will Aria? I wonder.

I finish my breakfast, and only seconds later, a young woman steps outside the hotel onto the sidewalk, a tote bag slung over her shoulder. She looks around, and for a split-second, our eyes meet. Even though it's nothing more than a coincidence, I'm glad for the baseball cap I'm wearing. She puts on shades and starts walking. I wait for a few seconds, my heart beating loudly now. Not that it should matter, but I realize that the photo I saw is likely a few years old. This version of Aria Bellini might be tired but is drop dead gorgeous.

It's bad timing for anything like that, and there's likely nothing in the cards. She'll be mad as hell once she figures out who I am. I have to be careful.

Without checking the actual bank account details, I know it will be a sum to get me ahead for a while.

But I'm not that easy. First, I want to know what Aria's European trip is all about.

—ℓℓ—

I follow her all day, not finding any proof that someone might be after her. She's exploring the sights, stopping for a coffee here and there, where she stares into nothing, looking as if she's contemplating deep thoughts. Like Tommy, she comes from a world of privilege, but maybe I'm fooling myself to think that knowing him allows me a window into her mind. It's different for women. I could only do what I was doing because while I was close to the family, I wasn't a Flynn, could stay outside the expectations.

Unlike Courtney. Even though everyone agreed to keep her largely in the dark regarding business matters, she was still expected to represent. Same for Sienna Caruso, or Aria.

How she stole away from it all, it's interesting and, I have to admit, admirable.

Maybe I have been admiring her a bit much.

Today, she's wearing a sundress with sneakers, somehow managing to look elegant and comfortable. I'm enjoying the surroundings, but it's hotter than I'd like, and I can feel my skin protest despite the copious amounts of sunscreen.

Aria looks happy and carefree, making me regret that I half-heartedly accepted this stupid job. Regardless, there are still things I need to find out before I deliver her home, like who are those business partners threatening her, and why Rome?

She makes a phone call on a burner. I remember from the original files that her cell phone was never recovered. Clearly, she has thought this through to some extent.

In the late afternoon, she takes the subway across town. I manage to get on the same train without her seeing me.

She's sitting a few seats in front of me, and I can see that her hair has some highlights. It looks soft to the touch. I can't indulge in some ill-fated crush though. Focus. It's too damn hot, or maybe that's just my inappropriate imagination regarding this young woman. I'm not sure where this is coming from. I dated a woman after college, for a few months. That's the extent of my experience, and I'm not sure I want to expand on that—or date anyone, for that matter. I want to go back to my cottage, the blessed familiarity of the fishing town and its scenic views, Keira's pub.

I want...

I abruptly abort the thought when she gets up. I do, too, and follow her out of the station and into a residential area. A few restaurants and cafés still line the streets, but there are fewer tourists around here. Is she going to see someone?

A secret lover her father didn't approve of?

If said lover existed, I'd say, good for her. Mixed in with the sentiment is another emotion, one I'm not quite ready to acknowledge yet. For Heaven's sake, I don't have time for this.

I follow her to an address with a large wooden door. There's a large brass door knocker, but also a few buzzers. She rings one of them, then talks through the intercom. Whoever the person on the other side is, they aren't receptive. She turns away in frustration, standing on the sidewalk indecisive. I pretend to look at the shop window of a bakery, watching her reflection walk away. Again, I follow.

Today, Aria doesn't do any sightseeing. Instead, she walks the streets rather aimlessly. I deduce from the slump of her shoulders that she expected different news.

Another surprise for me—I didn't expect the wave of emotion, the sudden urge to introduce myself to her, ask if she's okay. Maybe she didn't think this through. Tommy might have struggled, but he always had Rory and Ciara's support, even when he brought home Courtney.

Of course, Courtney gave them the desired grandson, but that's another, complicated story.

My phone rings, and I stop to look at it. Aria has stopped too, and she turns around. It's too late to hide, so I pretend to focus on my screen, as if I'm unaware of her presence. Even after what's presumably bad news, after another day of walking all day, she looks amazing, her expression pensive, pained even, as if there's a weight on her shoulders.

Maybe I am delusional, but I could think of ways to make it better. She looks my way, but I can't detect any recognition in her expression. I don't answer the call—it's Rory again. Instead, I make sure I stay at a reasonable distance.

It's at the subway station that I realize I've seen the man in the black t-shirt before. He walks with purpose, gaining on her.

I hasten my step as well, pretend I'm eager to get on the train first and squeeze between the two of them. He falls behind, doesn't get on the train. Am I paranoid? Aria doesn't seem to have noticed anything, but I won't take any chances.

I'm not going to let her out of my sight.

Maybe the danger she's in is greater than Bellini cutting her vacation short.

# Chapter Four

## Aria

Now, what? I can't tell if that single piece of information I had was accurate, or if I was lied to. By the person who gave it to me. Or the person who rudely told me to go away on the other side of that intercom.

What's worse, I can't shake the feeling that I'm being followed. By some guy, by a sexy woman with a perpetual frown, maybe I'm all making it up. Strangely enough, she looks a bit like the woman from the dream I had, only a few days ago in Paris. Coincidences, most likely.

I didn't want to admit it while I was still back in the States under Victor's watchful eye, but with so many miles between us, and me and Dad, I can face the growing fear that one of them might have something to do with my mother's disappearance. It might have been a heady mix of grief, curiosity, and aggravation with the lack of privacy that made me think about it first, but...What if?

On the other hand, what reason would he have? Mom always claimed that he was the love of her life. Or at least that's what I remember?

Do I? I came here to find answers, but so far, all I'm encountering are more questions.

Perhaps I have to give it more time, come back and plead my case again. Maybe the person who lives in that apartment has reason to worry if a Bellini knocks on their door.

The mystery remains.

I return to my hotel, take a shower and head back out, intending to battle that faint sense of dread. I need to have more of a plan for the next few weeks. I got away, fine. I found the place. I don't think there's a realistic reason to be afraid any longer. Mom had some friends here, but she never lived in Rome. Dad's family is from further South, and from what I've gathered, there has never been constant contact.

I have to be focused. This is not a vacation. It's my life now.

I choose a small restaurant on Via Margutta, dining on excellent pasta and a glass of red wine, feeling melancholic and a bit antsy. What if I can't find the answers? Could I make a life here, or elsewhere, maybe find someone to share it with? Could I work? Would I legally immigrate, or would I just have to travel from country to country and stay as long as the visa lasts?

If I went back home...No, I doubt I could ever give Dad an explanation he'd find satisfying, and besides, I don't want to find out how Victor feels about me ditching him.

I order tiramisu for dessert. When in Rome...I look up at the back wall, and there's a mirror. Sure enough, I see the redhead sitting in a booth, studying the menu. I haven't seen her come in, but I'm quite sure I've seen her before, and not just in my dreams.

The wine and distance from my overbearing environment have made me brave. I stare at her mirror image, waiting for her to realize I've made her. She's a bit older than I am, eight or ten years maybe, and...There's something about her that makes me shove my anger to the back of my mind. An air of intrigue and danger, and you would think I've had enough of both.

For a few seconds I can't help wondering, would it have been easier, if she had been the one tasked with guarding my person, and body? The thought is sending a shiver down my spine. It's a fantasy, of course. The lack of privacy would have gotten old after some time, no matter who had the job.

I am tired, and even though I've been surrounded by people all my life, it's been pretty lonely since losing my mother. To be honest, I don't want to think of my mother now.

My dessert arrives, and a few minutes later, the server brings me a shot of Amaretto, courtesy of the house. My eyes meet those of the mysterious woman, and I raise the shot glass, daring her.

She does the same with her wine glass.

Maybe, just maybe, she's interested in me? I doubt it though. A woman like her, if she had a personal interest, would have already approached me. The fact that she hasn't, is either complete coincidence, or she is working with that man, trying to do what? To keep me from talking to Mom's friends, finding out what happened the last time she came to visit them?

Maybe someone else is living there now. They could have moved away, or they might not know anything about her whereabouts. So why would Dad bother to send someone after them?

I see that she gets to her feet, so I do the same. I pay for my meal at the counter and head out quickly. She doesn't come out right away, probably still trying to uphold some sort of pretense. I walk along the street, telling myself that I need to take a breath.

This is what I wanted, hoped for, prepared for months. Me being by myself, free, able to exist without the constant looming shadow of Victor over me, metaphorically as a prospective husband, and literally. It's still exhilarating. The interest of an older attractive woman is, too, and maybe I should—

My thought is rudely interrupted when a car pulls up next to me, its left front tire screeching as the wheel embarks on the sidewalk. The back door opens, and a man I don't recognize grabs my arm, pulling me inside.

I struggle against his grip, strangely both shocked, and not—it's not like some part of me didn't see this coming.

Then there's a voice, and the sound of a click.

"Let her go, or you'll regret it." She sounds threatening, and at this moment, like an angel.

A split second is all she needs, and then my hand is in hers and we are running. Screeching tires again, then a gunshot. I nearly lose it there and then when I realize that whoever attempted this has no qualms about potentially killing innocent bystanders.

Even though the fear is all but choking me, my legs move as if by some miracle. I clutch the redheaded woman's hand and let her lead me through smaller streets, and eventually, back alleys too small for the car to follow us. The men in it might, though.

We aren't safe yet.

When I slow down, she turns to me, her face up close for the first time. I can see the concern in her green eyes. For someone a decade older than me, she's in excellent shape. I realize that I am not.

"Come on." Her tone is rather sympathetic, but there's no mistaking the urgency. I hear rapid footsteps, and I remember that these people have guns.

"I can't...breathe," I gasp.

She takes my hand again and holds on tightly as she drags me with her.

"There's a subway station over there. The next train will be here in a minute."

I realize that this is my only chance to escape.

Either that, or she's lying, and she's the one I should really fear. I'm going to take my chances.

# Chapter Five

## Saoirse

Aria sinks onto the plastic seat as I'm watching over her, making sure she doesn't faint, from exertion or shock. I see the two men on the platform, but they don't make it inside the train. We're safe for the moment, but neither of us can go back to their hotel room.

"Hey." I lay a hand on her shoulder. "You're okay."

"Speak for yourself," she jokes tiredly.

Until now, I had been wondering if Rory was exaggerating. Now I have definitive proof he wasn't. Someone was trying to abduct her here in Rome—that's elaborate, and I want to know who's behind this. Not just because it's part of my job to bring her home. I need to make sure she's safe first of all, and there are still a few steps to take.

"We'll stay on this line for a few stops, then change," I inform her. "You can relax for a bit. I have to make a call."

She nods, and for some reason I can't explain, I keep my hand on her shoulder. Aria doesn't protest. The contact calms both of us.

I nearly lose my patience when it takes my contact three rings to pick up, then it takes all the restraint I have left not to yell at her, but I manage. Before I can even think of getting us to an airport, I need to find us a safe location, where I can figure out the next step, and hopefully get Aria's side of the story.

"I'll arrange everything," my contact promises.

"Good. We'll be there in an hour max." I'm wondering if it's better to go back to Roma Termini, the central train station, and venture South, into the country maybe, but that bears its own risk. I conclude that for the moment, this will do. I end the call and study Aria, whose eyes are still wide from the terrifying experience of nearly getting abducted.

But it didn't happen. I was there in time. The thought fills me with deep relief.

"I found us a place to stay for now," I say.

"Who are you?" For someone who just survived a traumatic incident, her voice is surprisingly firm. Maybe she's still in denial, or, Aria, too, wasn't too surprised that it happened in the first place. Did her father share his suspicions, his business partners' threats with her?

"A friend," I say, cringing at the cliché. It's somewhat true, nonetheless. I'm the closest thing to a friend she has right now, and it had better count. "I'll tell you more once when we're there."

"And where is that?" she asks, a hint of frustration to her tone.

"Hey, I'm not the one kidnapping you. It was those gentlemen who tried."

That silences her, her beautiful features turning into an almost pout. It's adorable. No, that's not the right word. Distracting. I take a look around us, but people are mostly on their phones or staring into space, not paying attention to the two of us. This will work. I know because I took precautions before I got on the plane to Rome.

I didn't know I'd need them.

"This is our stop," I say. "Let's go."

There's a moment when we head up the stairs to change platforms when I worry she might try to run away from me. Maybe she's thinking about it, but a few minutes later we are on the next subway that will get us to our destination. I have to hope that Bellini's enemies, or whoever is behind this, don't have eyes and ears everywhere in this city. Who else could it be? A random attack on a tourist? It didn't look like that to me.

Can I rule out Bellini? I don't trust him, but if he wanted to send his own people after Aria, there would be no need to involve me. I believe he'd act more subtly than that. In any case, I assume that Aria will be able to answer some of those questions.

"It's not far," I assure her after we get out of the station and up on the street.

"Thank God for small favors." She sighs. "I suppose going back to the hotel is out of the question. Do you know who they were?"

"Not yet, but I'm going to find out. How about we settle in first, I make us something to eat, and we can talk? I'm Saoirse, by the way."

"Aria, but I think you knew that already."

I don't comment on it. That would be pointless.

I haven't been here before, but I researched the area as best as I could from afar, and so we make it to the safehouse in under forty-five minutes. This, too, is a residential area, but a bit more suburban, with the properties further apart.

Lucia lets us in.

"Let me know if you need anything," she says.

"This is great. Thank you."

"It's no problem," she assures me before she leaves.

Aria stood following the exchange silently, pensive. When I start to examine the rooms, she follows me as well. Everything is clean and accommodating. It will do perfectly until we've figured out where to go from here. In the bedroom upstairs, I point to the en suite.

"You can freshen up if you like. I'll check what's in the fridge and put something together."

"You cook?"

I'm not sure if I should be offended by that.

"Decently. You'll see."

Aria doesn't move, so I wait.

"We'll talk over dinner, I promise. Is there anything else?"

She hesitates.

"Tell me now. I want to get started. I'm kind of hungry."

"One bed? Really?"

Right. She had to bring that up. Her gaze is now challenging.

"That's your biggest problem right now, after two men tried to abduct you in broad daylight?"

I almost regret my words when she blanches at the reminder.

"I'll be in the kitchen."

"Okay," she says, softer. I've reached the door when she adds, "Thank you. For not letting that happen."

"You're welcome," I say before giving both of us some space. She can't leave the house without going past the kitchen in case she had planned that. We'll be all right for a few hours. But yes, one bed. I have the irrational idea that I could take her back home, or what is almost home, the cottage outside of Dublin.

First, I need to figure out what she's trying to find in Rome. And before that, I have to make us the promised dinner. My cooking style is fairly eclectic. I learned from Ciara, cookbooks and YouTube, and I have a pretty decent repertoire. Lucia must have gone grocery shopping the moment I called her, because there's fresh pasta, vegetables, and canned tomatoes. Some herbs and spices in the pantry. I can work with that.

I wish there was wine, but the circumstances require a clear head from both of us. Water will do.

When Aria comes back down, it smells amazing, and I can tell from her expression that she's pleasantly surprised. Or maybe just hungry. The last time I saw her eat, she had a small snack before lunch time.

"Sit down. It's ready."

"You're pretty bossy, Saoirse."

I'm not offended. In fact, it makes me laugh.

"I guess that's true. And you're probably used to more luxurious accommodations, but this is the best we can do at the moment."

"I'm not—" She stops herself. "It doesn't matter."

"Let's eat first." I set a plate in front of her and pour water for both of us. "Do you have any idea who those men were?"

Aria shakes her head. "I've never seen them before. But Victor must have sent them."

I've done my research. I know who he is, but I want her to tell the story in her own words.

"Tell me about this Victor, and why he'd want to kidnap you."

"Who else could it be? He's probably mad at me because I snuck away from him to come here. Dad...I wish he hadn't signed up on this, but I can't be sure. Victor is his head of security by the way."

"And you hurt his ego?"

She laughs a little. Beautiful My heart flutters.

Not the time. Not that there would ever be a time for this. The thought of getting involved with another woman, this particular woman, is scary. I have a job to do. This inexplicable need, out of nowhere, is scary, and I can't let emotions distract me from the priority to keep her safe.

"I suppose I did, but there's more. I don't know if you can imagine...I'll inherit the company someday, and there's a lot of money involved. Dad doesn't think I can handle it. He wants me to marry a man who will take over, and I've so far neglected to tell him that's not in the cards."

"Why not?"

Believe it or not, arranged marriages are still a thing in these circles. But wanting your daughter to be married to Victor Orlov takes a special kind of evil. It makes me less and less eager to hand Aria over to her father. So, it's him behind the abduction? Or has Bellini made even more powerful enemies?

"First of all, Victor." She shudders. "You have no idea what my life has been like. My mother went missing when I was thirteen...I feel stupid. Why don't you tell me what you already know, and who sent you? That would make it easier."

I study her, trying to gauge what her reaction to a sliver of truth would be.

"This is delicious, by the way. You win. You really can cook. I wish it came with a nice red."

"You and me both, but there are some other things we have to get out of the way first. All right. I got word that some of your father's recent business partners have been unsatisfied with a deal that fell through, and that they were planning to get to him through you."

"Bullshit," she says harshly. "He doesn't care about me that much, and people who do business with him know that. Siccing those bodyguards on me 24/7, it's for show. I know Mom loved him, but...He wants me to marry Victor. I could never." She's on her feet before I can answer.

"We can end this right here. If you're working for my Dad, tell him I'm not coming back. And I won't marry Victor, or any man he wants to parade in front of me, because I'm a lesbian."

I hold up a hand, though I'm secretly thrilled with this information.

"Hold on. If I was working for your dad, why would I risk my hide to rescue you and get us a safehouse where we can enjoy Italian cuisine?"

She's still irritated, though a bit of that fight is leaving her, because indeed, it wouldn't make much sense. She doesn't need to know everything at this point.

"I'm not sure I got all the information either. Why don't we work together to figure this out?"

To my relief, she sits back down.

"You want a mystery, Saoirse? I can give you one."

Aria Bellini is many things. She's also one of the few people who pronounced my name correctly on the first try, and she seems to like saying it.

It's not the worst start.

# Chapter Six

## Aria

I don't know what to think, about what happened today, about this irritating, gorgeous woman who has somehow taken over my life. I'm not naive. She must have some stake in this—no one is completely unselfish. At least, she seems sympathetic to my struggles, and what's even more interesting, she has resources.

"I can't go back," I repeat. "I think Dad would lock me in and never let me out again. He's been paranoid ever since Mom disappeared. Maybe that's how you heard the story of his business partners. He has enemies, sure, but I never felt like I was in danger from any of them. His security guards, that's a different story."

"Did anyone of them ever touch you? Victor?"

Behind the calm tone, I sense the anger blazing, and it's just one more piece of the puzzle that makes me want to trust Saoirse. For sure, I believe she's more trustworthy than Victor and what's left of my own family.

"No," I say, aware of her relief. I'm relieved too. I got away in time. "It might have come to that though. I don't know. I had a bad feeling. Anyway, I never intended to stay in Rome for a long time." I pick up the tote bag I've been carrying around with me all day. It's a miracle I haven't lost it with everything that's happened. I'd be screwed. Even more screwed.

Saoirse watches me cautiously when I open it.

"I don't have a gun. All I have is an address…This was where my mother was last seen."

"That was when, fourteen, fifteen years ago?"

"Fourteen," I say, irrationally pleased that she gauged my age correctly. "I know it's a long shot, but it's all I have."

"The address you visited earlier."

"Yes. But the person living there refused to talk to me."

"Maybe the one you want moved away?"

"No, there was a couple, a man and a woman Mom was friends with. She talked about them sometimes. I think they got divorced, and he left, but the woman still lives there. I recognized the name."

"It could still be a dead end," Saoirse suggests.

"Maybe, but in order to find out, I have to go back."

"No way. It's too dangerous."

"Excuse me? I expressed my gratitude, and I'll make sure to pay you back for your expenses. That's it. You can't keep me here."

Her expression is calm, and much too patient now.

"I don't need any money from you, but I don't think you'll want to take your chances with those guys."

Fuck, she's right. Did she have to point it out? My great adventure didn't last long, I'm once again stressed as hell, ready to snap, yell at her…kiss her. Where did that come from? I might have, before, if we had met under different circumstances. This is already too messy.

"I could be anywhere right now. I need to have some answers. You don't know what it's like."

"You're right."

"They didn't come after me when I went there. I don't think anyone knows. But it's my only chance to find out what happened to her!"

She is silent for a few beats.

"I understand that. Still, it's too dangerous."

"Why, I have you now, don't I? You did a pretty great job protecting me."

Is it the light, or did I make her blush? I can't help smiling, even though I was angry with her five seconds ago. "Look, I'm not your responsibility, but I promise you, if you help me out one more time, and we can see Beatrice, I'll do whatever you think is necessary."

There's still a missing piece. Why did she get involved in the first place?

"Please. There's strength in numbers, right? All I want is for her to tell me what happened the last time she talked to Mom. Maybe it's nothing, and then I have to live with it, but maybe we could find out where she went from there..."

"It's a bad idea. We should wait it out here for a few days and then..."

"And then what? You're going to be my shadow wherever I go? Forget about it. I told you, whatever story you heard, it's probably Dad being paranoid. It's more important that he doesn't know where I am."

Saoirse contemplates this, before she says,

"Do you think he had something to do with your mother's disappearance?"

I sink into the chair, deflated. All of today's exhaustion and fear seems to be coming down on me at once.

"I don't want to think that. I don't know. Who sent you?"

"Like I said, a friend. You don't have to worry. I'll make sure you're safe. If necessary, from your father."

I shouldn't, but I believe her. The fiery delivery feels genuine, and it's also...hot. I wouldn't mind being stuck here with her a little while longer if I wasn't on that mission. And as long as my mind is occupied with that, and her, I won't have to decide where to go next, question whether there's any place for me that would be completely safe.

"So, we're going tomorrow?"

"Very early tomorrow," she says. "You'll have one shot, and if this woman doesn't want to talk, that's it."

That will most definitely not be it, but I know not to press my luck, and nod.

"Thank you. And...I was wondering...You found me."

"I did."

"So, it's something you're good at. I can pay you. Hell, I'll pay you more than that friend, if you help me find her."

Her sympathetic gaze borders on pity, and I almost get angry again. However, I have thought about the possibilities. Some of them worse than others. Women go missing and are never found again. It happens more than anyone thinks, and often enough the explanation is something horrifying. I choose to believe that as long as we don't know for sure, there's still hope.

We have to move fast. She sort of confirmed that Dad and Victor will not let this go easily, unless that far-fetched story about the business partners turns out to be true.

"I still don't need your money. I'll see what I can do, but you have to trust me, okay?"

Like that's so easy for me right now. I suppose she does have a point. She didn't need to intervene, and if she hadn't, who knows where I would be now?

"I'm going to clean up," she announces. "After that, tell me everything you have so far."

"I told you, there's only the address..."

"Everything you remember from that time. What you were told, by whom, every detail can be important. You want to do this, we better get to it right away."

Still no wine.

"I can help you," I offer. "And I'll tell you what I know."

# Chapter Seven

## Saoirse

Between dinner and some serious talk, I excuse myself and go up to the bedroom, trusting she won't run away now. What a dilemma she has created for me. I am resourceful, but even with my contacts, can I solve the decade-old case of a missing woman? What am I getting myself into?

Forget about peace and closure in the Irish countryside. The Flynns used to be a blessing in my life, until they became a curse.

Speaking of which.

"Why don't you return my calls?" Rory asks, sounding annoyed. Well, I am too.

"You were the only one who knew. How come a couple of minions tried to kidnap Aria today, when I'm the one that's supposed to bring her home safely?"

"What? I don't know anything about that." He is so indignant, I almost believe him. But Rory hasn't gotten to where he is, or at least was, before he let a corrupt cop into his business, because of a lack of intelligence. He knows how to play the game.

"Don't you? They were Bellini's, weren't they?"

"I don't know what you're talking about. Just do the God-damn job, you hear me?"

This gives me pause. Until now, he knew better than to talk to me like that.

"Excuse me?" I say coldly, and there's a pause on the other hand. Rory clears his throat.

"I didn't mean it like that. Come on, Saoirse, it's me. Antonio is certain that the girl is in danger, and it sounds like he was right about that. Just bring her home. That's all he's asking."

"What if she doesn't want to go home? She's not a little girl."

Oh, most definitely. She's not.

"Don't make a mistake. Aria is well aware of her obligations. Now's not the time to act foolish. Get on a plane."

"I'll get back to you," I say, and hang up again.

Aria won't be happy if I change my mind again, but going back to the apartment of her mother's friends might be a big risk. On the other hand, getting closer to the truth might give her a bargaining chip in case Bellini senior doesn't accept her decision to step away from his terrible legacy.

When I come downstairs, she's sitting on the sofa. It's not big enough to stretch out on, hence the one-bed situation. It's not big enough to stay far away from each other either, but I take my chances.

"You know, for a while, I was scared to even think about it. I didn't want to remember a time before, because we were happy, and one day it just ended. I can't explain it."

"You were only thirteen," I say softly. "It must have been traumatic."

Aria shrugs. "It was terrible, but how Dad reacted, it was worse. He simultaneously became unavailable and at the same time, made sure I wouldn't be alone. When I was in high school, they all but came to the bathroom with me. The kids made fun of me because they thought I imagined myself to be some kind of celebrity with bodyguards. I just hated it."

"I can imagine." I wince, thinking that I definitely can. It was easier for Tommy, because we'd been friends before, but I could always tell that Courtney wasn't too happy with my presence. Of course, she also worried I'd steal her husband.

*Moving on.*

"How did you find out about the address?"

"I secretly hired a PI."

"You are full of surprises." I mean it as a compliment.

"Look who's talking," she returns.

"Okay, back to the matter at hand. The PI, that's the only thing they found out?"

"She, and yes, pretty much. Mom went to visit her friends, was supposed to arrive back in the States the following week. The couple took her to the airport, but she was never seen again."

"Kind of like you," I can't help saying. This is strange. Now, Rome is not more or less violent than your average big city, so the incidents that keep happening to this family are...bad luck? It's reasonable to think that the couple might know more, or that Bellini had a hand in all of this.

I take in her tired expression, feeling sad for her. Aria has a lot on her plate already. Has she considered that her father might have had a hand in her mother's disappearance? That he could have gotten her killed? Or did her so-called friends betray her?

I can't blame her for wanting the truth. It's only complicated by the fact that her father wants her back home. Perhaps I gave the Flynns a pass too often because they had been generous and welcoming when I felt like I had no place to go. With a bit of distance, it's not so hard to see the similarities. How they dismissed Courtney, were already planning a future for her young son.

41

"But I didn't vanish..." She shivers. "Thanks to you, that is. Do you think...What if they weren't her friends after all? But that doesn't make sense. They didn't know I was coming."

"I think you're right. Organizing an abduction between the moment you rang the doorbell, and when you left the restaurant, seems a bit quick. Yet, we can't rule out that someone doesn't want you to know what happened to your mother."

There, I said it. If I truly believe this, then everything points to Bellini, doesn't it? Does Rory know?

I won't have a choice. I'll have to talk to him in person at some point, separate fact from fiction. I truly thought finding out who killed Tommy would change something. I didn't imagine Rory's renewed connections with the Italian mafia would include someone ruthless like Bellini. Does Bellini have something on him? Maybe I should call my FBI contact, or Sienna Caruso. Either one of them might have some information for me. In the meantime, I have accepted another job, to solve another mystery. Unreasonably so, but it looks like I can't say no to her.

I'm aware of her gaze on me, questioning.

"Why did you bring me here?" she asks.

"You know why," I say, holding her gaze.

"I'm glad you didn't let those men take me. Arranging a safehouse is going above and beyond, Saoirse."

"It was the sensible thing to do. I don't want anything to happen to you."

"Why?" she whispers.

Yes, why? Because I have felt drawn to her the moment I opened that picture Rory sent me? Because I carry a lot of baggage when it comes to protecting the ones I care about, and failing at it? I was told to stay away that night, by Tommy, and by Rory. No one blamed me like I blamed myself, but that's over now. Forget about that money in my bank account. I work for no one.

Once I make sure Aria has everything she needs I'll go back to that cottage, see if I can make a life in the country of my ancestors...

Why?

"I couldn't handle it," I tell the naked truth and lean forward, desperate to keep a minimum of control in this rapidly spiraling situation. I've been fooling myself. The moment our lips meet, I'm gone. Hers are soft and warm, and if Aria is surprised by the kiss, there's no indication because she pulls me to her and holds on for dear life. The heat is too much, too soon. I can't deal with this much want when I have to protect her at the same time, figure out those different strands of truth. I pull back.

"That's a bad idea," I say, self-consciously aware of my breathless tone.

Aria licking her lips nearly undoes me. I could abandon all reason and responsibility and have her right here on the too small couch. It wouldn't take much. I can't.

"My life has been a series of bad ideas, mostly those of other people," she says with a hint of amusement. "Those scary men notwithstanding, lately, it's been amazing. This is the most me I've been in forever. Part of it is because I'm finally getting closer to figuring out what happened to my mom. The other part...Well, you felt it too, didn't you?"

I can't help smiling, even though much is tricky about this situation. And dangerous. I guess we can have a small respite until tomorrow morning.

"That's not the point, is it? Let's take it one day at a time. Did you have any plans beyond solving your mother's disappearance?"

She sinks back into the cushions, but is still far too close.

"Not much," she admits. "I don't want to go back. Being here, it's ridiculous to think about, but I'm pretty sure Dad is serious about those wedding plans. If it's not Victor, it will be another guy he chooses, so his legacy is protected." She makes a face, and I sympathize, so much.

It's no longer just about making sure she doesn't fall into the hands of those mysterious business partners, or Bellini's men, or whoever the wannabe kidnappers were. I can't stand the thought of Bellini selling her off to one of his henchmen. I won't let it happen.

"It should be your choice," I say.

"Oh, I agree. This is why I guess I'll be on the run for a little while longer."

I think of the cottage, the life I've been dreaming about.

"I'll be with you as long as you need me."

"And your friend...?"

"Forget about him. I work only for myself."

The smile brightens her face.

"Since you don't want money, perhaps we could think of something else."

I can't help it, I'm laughing. But the mere suggestion makes the heat between us rise again. One of us might have to sleep on the couch after all, and I suspect it won't be Princess Bellini.

# Chapter Eight

## Aria

Have I lost my mind? My father would certainly think so, but he doesn't know what's going on, hell, he doesn't know me. Never has, except for maybe when I was very young. My mind is in disarray, the latent fear of what we might uncover, confusion over how there came to be a "we" in this, my escape...

Saoirse.

I don't want to stop and think about possible mistakes, danger, the future ahead. Perhaps it's the recent danger that plays a role in my emotions and behavior, but there's something deeper, undeniable that goes beyond me lusting after her. I am, there's no denying.

I've had a few one-night-stands before, quick encounters to satisfy a curiosity, because my circumstances didn't allow more. I fooled the guards. I fooled Dad, but it was always a dangerous game. I risked the most when I got that nude painting done. I couldn't risk bringing it home, so it's probably still somewhere in the studio of that gorgeous but aloof painter, Sela Andras.

Saoirse is equally as assertive, not to mention gorgeous—even more so to me because she is fiery, intense in a different way. She makes me feel safe. Even when I had the strange dream, which must have been from subconsciously noticing her, and then when I thought she was following me…Wait, was she following me in Paris?

Very little of this story makes sense, but when we get ready for the night, the bed we'll share seems very small all of a sudden. I try to chalk it all up to the situation we've shared, the rush…Saoirse seems less bothered by it as she slips under the sheet.

"Get in," she says. "We have an early start tomorrow."

Like I don't know that. Meeting my mother's friends has been a huge part of my motivation to plan all of this. I feel like I'm getting sidetracked, by strange men coming after me—or not so strange?

By her.

I still only have a t-shirt and panties to sleep in, hyper-aware of my scarce state of dress, but it can't be helped. I bought a few clothes in Paris, but I left most of them in the hotel room.

"I should have done a load of laundry," I say in the darkness. Saoirse turns to me. I can make out her shape. She's wearing summer PJs, matching top and bottom. I wish I could reach out and touch her, but she hit the brakes hard after that kiss, and I feel like it wouldn't be welcome.

"There's time tomorrow," she says. "Or I can lend you something."

I sense the unspoken question, and explain, "I couldn't bring any more than a change of clothes with me. Victor would have been suspicious."

"It's not a problem. You should sleep now. Tomorrow we'll give this one more try."

"What if it doesn't work?"

All of a sudden, my heart is beating loudly, and not from excitement. The term dead end rings uncomfortably true, scary and realistic. But if I had been realistic about my options, I would have never made it here, would I?

Saoirse reaches out to touch my hand, and just like that, she brings me back from the brink of harrowing doubts. Even though I've been surrounded by personal security for so long, none of them could ever make me feel like I was secure, like nothing bad could happen to me.

Saoirse makes me feel that way, and I cherish the novelty of this emotion.

"We'll cross that bridge when we come to it," she says. Coming from her, it doesn't sound like a platitude, but the truth. She's a woman who always has a plan. And she promised to be around. I'll hold her to it.

—ele—

I make a faint sound in protest when Saoirse wakes me. The day is barely dawning, and I'm still exhausted even though I slept surprisingly well.

"Come on. We need to go."

I sit up and suppress a yawn, startled when I realize she's already fully dressed.

"I have something for you to wear. Get ready, and we can grab something to eat on the way back," she promises.

I'm hungry now, and in need of caffeine, but I don't want to hold us back, or worse, sound like an ungrateful brat. I haven't fully processed what happened yesterday, or since I arrived in Europe, for that matter. Saoirse obviously knows what she's doing, but the men that tried to make me disappear were likely armed. They could have hurt her.

I do as she tells me, wash up in the small bathroom and put on the clothes she's handed me.

A minute later, we are out the door. There's a car parked at the back of the house, but we don't take it, head to the subway instead.

"We can take a cab later. Not all the way here, but close enough."

We are both wearing capris and shirts now, baseball caps to complete the tourist outfit that came with the safehouse.

No detours. We go straight to the metro station, then take the train back into the city. Change trains twice. Saoirse's expression is one of tense focus, and I'd find this incredibly sexy, if so much didn't hinge on this mission. On us making it to safety.

Doubts are beginning to creep along the edges of my mind. What if this was a terrible mistake? What if I have put us both in danger? But what's the alternative? Hide out in that house for the next few months? There's a part of me that doesn't mind, but Rome still is too close to yesterday's incident. It would probably be a good idea to choose another country.

Is that what Saoirse meant when she said she'd stay? Anywhere I'd go? I've known this woman for less than forty-eight hours, and already I'm depending on her. That's either incredibly lucky or incredibly foolish. Perhaps both.

We have reached the last stop. From here, we walk to the apartment building where I rang the doorbell yesterday.

"Let me do this," Saoirse says, and before I can protest, she rings the doorbell. Well. I got that far too. The same woman answers, and my jaw drops when Saoirse starts speaking in somewhat accented, but fluent Italian. I understand some of it, but by far not enough. For all of Dad's pride in our heritage, he didn't consider language all that important. Something about a gas leak?

It's a lie, and a blatant one, but it does get us into the building. We go up the stairs to the door #7. The woman has opened the door a fraction but leaves the chain lock in place.

I don't blame her. We sure don't look like we come from the city. What's more, she looks younger than I'd expect a friend of mom's to be.

"It's you again," she says accusingly.

"Beatrice? I need to talk to you about my mom. Please. It's important."

"I don't know who you are, or your mother, and I don't care. Please, leave me alone."

"I'm Aria Bellini," I repeat. "My mom's Marina Cacciatore. She came here to this place when I was thirteen and never returned."

"I don't know anything about that," she says. "Is that all?"

"Aria came all the way here. You could at least hear her out." Saoirse's tone, less desperate, seems to have an impact.

The woman closes the door, there's the sound of her removing the chain, and she opens it again.

"Come on in."

It happens so fast I don't even have time to breathe or be shocked—again—when she slams the door shut and pulls a gun on us.

"Who the hell are you?"

My gaze flickers to Saoirse who raises her hand—doesn't she have a gun too? I'm just too accustomed to being around people who carry. Her expression is calm though, and I realize with an emotion between dread and admiration that she has handled a situation like this before. Maybe even more than once. Well, she's here and alive, that must mean something.

"She told you, her name is Aria, and she's looking for her mom. I'm Saoirse. I'm just here to help. All we have is this address. You are Beatrice?"

The woman shakes her head.

"Please, put down the gun. We don't mean to harm you. All we want is answers."

"You're not the first," she says bitterly.

"Did someone threaten you?"

"Not stupid, I have to give you that." She lowers the gun, and I take a deep breath. "Beatrice is my mother. Marina came to visit her and my father. I told the other guy I wasn't home that day, and that I don't know anything. I don't even know where my parents are at this moment. It's for their own safety."

"I'm sorry about all this. I didn't mean to cause you trouble, and I don't think Mom wanted that for your parents. I just want to know what happened."

She slumps into an armchair and gestures for us to sit. Instead, Saoirse steps to the window, keeping an eye on the street below.

"I'm Emilia, by the way. Like I said, I told those guys I wasn't there. I don't know if they believed me, or what they would have done if my boyfriend hadn't arrived. We have increased security since. We installed cameras, so I saw you yesterday. They haven't been back, but I always feared they might be."

"Wait, when did that happen?" There's an edge to Saoirse's tone.

"A few weeks ago, why?"

Our eyes meet, and I'm sure my surprise shows on my face. How is that possible? I was so careful with my research. If Victor or Dad had gotten wind of it, I don't think I would have made it onto the plane to Paris.

"We've been followed too," Saoirse says. "If I had to take a wild guess, I'd say it's all related. What did your parents say about Marina's visit?"

"That she wanted to leave her husband. That she couldn't stand it any longer, but she couldn't leave her daughter—I guess that's you—alone. I heard her say it. Looks like she changed her mind."

Or someone found her first. I shudder. None of it makes sense. If someone tried to hold her back, if they got to her, who are the people still looking for Mom? And if she made it out, does that mean she's alive somewhere? I'm once again excited and terrified, and I've almost forgotten that Beatrice's daughter waved a gun in our faces only minutes ago.

There's another emotion I can't quite process yet. Was there ever a moment when she thought about taking me with her? So many people think I'm lucky, having grown up in the wealthy Bellini family. I would have given it up in a heartbeat, had I only known how unhappy my mother was. I could have been with her instead.

"It doesn't look like they have found her yet," I say. That means, perhaps, we could? And what would I say to her, fourteen years later?

"If that's all, I'd like you to leave now."

"Do you have any idea where Marina might have gone?"

"No one told me. I guess they wanted to protect me too."

"Do your parents own property?"

"Are you kidding me? I haven't spoken to them in months. If your father is as much of an asshole as I hear he is, good for Marina that she got away, but I don't want to get in the middle of this any more that I already have. I hate that my parents aren't safe because of it. If you could—"

"Hang on a second," Saoirse says, something about her tone startling both me and Emilia. "Is there another way out of here other than through the front door?"

"What the hell?" Emilia sounds resigned. "Yes, there is. Come on."

"I don't want to alarm you, but you might want to take that gun with you."

Emilia has a light coat, her purse—and the gun—on her only seconds later as she leads us along the corridor to another wooden door that opens to a stairwell. As we hurry down, we can hear footsteps in the hallway, then fists knocking on the door, shouting voices.

We make it down and out into a back alley.

Where to now?

"You can come with us," Saoirse offers. Emilia purses her lips. "Why would I? I don't know you either."

"You'd be someplace safe until we figure out what's going on. And we need your car."

I might have been pretty clever getting out of the country the way I did, but there's something about the way Saoirse anticipates situations. I might be about to crash sometime soon, but for the moment, I'm in awe.

# Chapter Nine

## Saoirse

Once again, I ignore a call from Rory. I'm aware this can't go on forever. Another person to take care of, though Aria remains my priority. It seems like Emilia can take care of herself, but we needed that car, and I didn't want to risk leaving her fending for herself.

Aria is surprisingly still holding up—I wouldn't blame her if she came to the end of her rope sometime soon after the constant confrontations, and recent revelations, part unsettling, part hopeful.

Apparently, like Aria, her mother Marina took the chance when she could. What we don't know is if there was ever a chance to take Aria with her. I remember Aria saying that her mother told her Bellini was the love of her life. Exaggeration? Lie? Was it the truth at some point? Either way, the closer we get, the more we have to brace ourselves that things aren't what they seem to be. I almost laugh at my train of thought. We.

It's pretty clear at this point.

The peace I hoped to find was short-lived, but I must see this through now. Keep my promise.

I glance over at Aria, and she gives me a grateful smile.

Safe once more.

Soon, we should talk about where to go from here.

—ella—

I made a judgment call taking Emilia with us, because I think she might be in danger from the same people who are looking for Aria and Marina, and because I'm fairly sure she hasn't told us the whole story yet.

We don't have a lot of time. Aria won't like it, but I'd prefer if we stayed on the move, got out of Rome, or even out of the country. Marina could be anywhere by now, but I'm willing to give it one last shot.

"What now?" Emilia asks when we park in front of the safe-house. "You really think you can hold them off?"

"Don't worry about it. This location is secure for now," I say. "I don't know about you, but neither of us has had breakfast, so let's eat." I also hope that she's going to feel a bit less reluctant to talk. Everyone is trying to protect themselves, I get that.

But we have a common enemy. If we play our cards right, she won't have to worry about her parents either, though that's still a long shot.

Emilia shrugs at that. "I guess I'm invited."

"You and your parents were the last ones to see my mom alive," Aria says, as if it only occurs to her now. Something in Emilia's gaze softens.

"I know this is painful," she says. "At least I hear from my parents every once in a while."

I definitely think she has more to tell us.

Inside, I prepare the coffee and take out some food. Fortunately, there's everything we need for a comforting breakfast. The coffee is dark and strong.

Rory is calling again.

This time, I text him.

*Stop calling*, I say. *Things are under control. We'll talk later.*

*Where is Aria? You can't mess with Antonio.*

*I'm not messing with anyone. Tell him to call off the hounds. Aria is not going back.* I delete the last sentence and hit "send" when I see Emilia standing in the doorway.

"Can I help you with anything?" she asks.

"No, thanks. Not breakfast, anyway. But it's really important to Aria we find out what happened. If you have any idea where her mother could be..."

"I told you, I don't know. If my parents helped her get away, I have no idea. I was just a kid too, remember? I never asked for any of this."

"Neither did Aria. We want the same thing, Emilia."

"Do we? Yesterday I was minding my own business. Now I'm on the run with a couple of clueless Americans. I kind of know now how my parents felt. They just wanted to help, and look what happened."

"Emilia..."

"You're taking an awful long time with that coffee," Aria, who has joined us, says. "I'm starving."

"Coffee is done." No cappuccino, but I could manage a dark strong brew with the machine. "The rest is coming along." I point to the table where I laid out plates and utensils. The pastries are storebought, but that will have to do for now. No beans or sausages, but I've whipped up a few eggs.

"Thank you."

"Yes, thank you," Emilia echoes. "This is all insane, but I appreciate the way you handled things. You could have just stolen my car. I assume."

I can't help the wry smile. "I could have."

Aria glances at me with a mix of confusion and admiration. I am close to being overwhelmed, so I can only imagine what it feels like from her perspective.

"Anyway. Let's eat."

Over breakfast, Aria fills Emilia in on her recent days, and I can tell that Emilia is relaxing slightly. Right. I'm the one who has the most to hide, including my account balance. But it's Rory who made the transfer into an account I never even accessed, so I don't see a problem there.

There's no way I'll hand Aria over to Bellini, no matter where we have to go.

I try to ask unobtrusive questions, though Emilia rolling her eyes tells me she's on to me.

"I'm really sorry. I told you everything I know. Marina wanted to leave, that's all she said. My parents drove her to the airport. I didn't go, so I don't know what happened. They never said."

"And you never asked, even after there were threats?"

"It didn't occur to me. I didn't want to make things worse either. Do you really think I'd enjoy stalling you?"

"I didn't mean anything." Not entirely true, but let's leave it at that for the moment. "I'm sorry. More coffee anyone?"

"Me, please," Aria says. "I didn't get to sleep a lot."

I think she'll be walking on the ceiling if she drinks any more, but all of a sudden the air in the room is heavy with suggestion, and I see that Emilia is barely suppressing a smile, getting the entirely wrong idea. I couldn't care less about what she thinks, though this is a sad reminder that innuendo is all we'll have for now. Anything else...It's not safe. If we don't manage to get more out of Emilia, any clue, we'll have to leave soon. I don't know that Aria is fully aware of that.

I call Lucia and ask her to keep an eye on Emilia's apartment. She can't stay here forever, but once she's gone, Aria and I won't be able to stay either, so it's all about precautions now.

"I need to talk to Aria for a moment," I say. "Please, give me your phone."

Emilia gives me an incredulous glance. "Excuse me?"

"I promise you, I won't go through it. But you can't call anyone."

She groans but produces it out of her purse. "Last time I spoke to my parents was five months ago. The number doesn't exist any longer."

"Like I said..."

"Yeah, whatever."

I take Aria's hand and steer her to the bedroom where I close the door.

"Maybe you should have taken her car keys too?" she suggests.

"I doubt that she's going to run. She can't stay with us forever either. Someone will get suspicious, her parents, her boyfriend. I'm going to tell her to go see him tomorrow and get in touch with the police. I'll provide her with a name."

"Okay..." she says, sounding unsure.

"It's better that way. And for what it's worth, I'm sorry, but I think she's told us everything she knows. Lucia will make sure it's okay for her to go back. That's all we can do for now."

"Where does that leave us?" Her soft-spoken question has multiple implications. "We'll hang out here? Wait to see if anything else comes up?"

"Aria." Almost against my will, I step forward, lift my hand to brush over her hair.

"This is it. I've asked around, we talked to Emilia, you heard what she said. If there's anything more to investigate, it will take time and resources. I'm not saying we can't ever revisit it, but now is not the time. Once Emilia is gone, this location won't be secure anymore."

"Where will we go?"

I can't seem to bring myself to break the contact.

"Somewhere safer," I promise her.

"Why didn't she take me with her?" Aria wonders out loud, sounding very young all of a sudden.

I pull her close.

I wish I knew.

# Chapter Ten

## Aria

There's no temptation whatsoever that night when Saoirse insists that Emilia sleeps in the bed with me, while she is risking neck and back injury on that tiny couch. I assume she won't be sleeping much anyway. Neither will I.

Emilia doesn't seem to have such problems. Within minutes, she is snoring softly, but I can't find sleep other than a few restless confusing minutes at a time.

Eventually, I give up and walk over into the living room. Saoirse is frowning at her phone.

"Bad news?" I ask softly. As if it could get worse.

Well, at least we're still here together. Still free.

She puts the phone away.

"No. Don't worry about it."

I decide to trust her. She doesn't sound worried, just contemplative. I sit down next to her, and, like drawn by an invisible force, lean towards her. She wraps an arm around me, and I snuggle into her embrace. I had other things on my mind earlier, but this is what I need now.

"I bet you didn't have any of this on your bingo card."

She gives a wry laugh. "I'm usually pretty good at expecting every possible scenario, but no. You're right."

"I can't leave Rome," I say, not facing her. "I've been obsessing about this for years. Made the plan. I can't go until we find what happened to her...or find her."

Up until a few hours ago, I didn't even know that was a possibility.

"What if she doesn't want to be found?"

I thought about that too. There's a chance she wasn't just running from Dad, but her entire life. Including me.

"I don't know."

Saoirse is softly stroking my hair, and a part of me is disappointed and irritated, mostly with myself. I don't want to be in this state. I seriously overestimated myself thinking I could solve the case, fend off all enemies and seduce a beautiful older woman...Turns out I can't do any of it. But I won't marry Victor either, she and I have decided this, and it's got to count for something.

"Where would we go?" I ask.

"I'm making inquiries, just in case," she says. "We have several options. It's safer if I don't tell you until we are actually on a train or plane. Of course, eventually...You might find more answers at home."

"No. Absolutely not." I sit up straight as I say it, seeking her gaze. She can't be serious, after everything I've told her! "Dad has connections. If he finds out I did all of this on purpose...He's never going to forgive me. I don't want to know what he's going to do. He can make my life hell, and yours too. I don't want that to happen."

"I understand. It was just a thought."

"No." I shake my head. "It's up to you if you want to stay."

"Aria." Her tone is warm and pleading now, and I can't resist. "Of course I'll stay. We'll head out tomorrow. Emilia can drop us off at the train station. I'm sorry we can't do more here, not at the moment anyway. They've tried twice already."

"I'm aware," I concede with a sigh. "And yes, I'd like to be someplace where I can stay for a while, buy clothes and actually wear them."

Her soft smile warms my heart, and other parts. I wish Emilia wasn't still sleeping in that bed, or that the couch was a little bigger. That I was a little braver.

I need to chase all those thoughts from my head, most of them largely irrational, that Mom might have never wanted me, that she was looking for a way out right from the start.

That someone might have found her already. That she could be—"

"We'll get you some clothes. I promise. Now, you should go back to sleep."

"You're not sleeping," I point out.

"I can sleep on the train. Go, get some rest."

She kisses me on the lips, a mere brush of lips against lips, another promise and a tease.

I have no choice but to oblige.

At this point, I'll do whatever it takes to keep her with me.

Because she actually knows what to do when trouble shows up.

And because I'm holding on to the faint chance that she changes her mind about taking that chance.

# Chapter Eleven

## Saoirse

It was supposed to be easy. Assess the situation, make a decision, move on. I'm far away from home—either home—and there's no solution in sight. At the moment, just another escape. It's a small blessing that money isn't a problem at this point, even if I never touch that dubious sum from a man I certainly don't want to owe.

Emilia, at least, is grateful for everything I've arranged. As planned, she will drop us off at the station. We have a quick coffee at the house, then we are on our way.

It pains me that I can't take Aria to the cottage, pretend we're just two strangers who met on a European trip and were attracted to each other, now exploring the possibilities.

Much like Tommy and Courtney. It doesn't look like I can get away from the Flynns anytime soon.

I suppress a yawn when we say goodbye to Emilia and walk into the central train station.

We brought a few clothes, mostly mine, in backpacks, nothing too heavy. We also left Aria's tote bag purse behind, which she did with a bit of regret, but it's better if we make a run for it as inconspicuously as possible. I keep an eye on her and our surroundings as I pay cash for the tickets, and then for a breakfast to go that we will eat on the train.

"So, Germany," Aria remarks. "You think that's going to be far enough?"

"For now," I say. It takes a long time to travel by train, but I want to avoid planes for now. On the bright side, our pursuers don't know our itinerary. I want to go back to Munich, sleep, and get all the way to Hamburg the next day. Stay on the move but be in a bigger city from where we could catch a plane home if the need arises. I think that will be unavoidable at some point, even if Aria doesn't see it that way yet. For now, I'll make do with my European contacts and the skills I've acquired guarding the secrets and persons of the Flynn family.

I choose seats for us in an open-plan car where we won't face anyone. At this point, we can't be too careful, even though Lucia and Emilia have strict instructions.

We are close to departure time when I see the men on the platform and suppress a curse.

"Keep your head down," I say. "I mean that literally. Now."

Aria's initial confusion morphs into alarm, but she does as I say, rummaging for something in her backpack, while I also duck. The doors close with an unmistakable sound, and we are on our way. I see the two men conferring, their expressions showing their anger, and take a deep breath. That was close. Too damn close, multiple times, and it doesn't make sense. Does Bellini really have so many resources? Unless he always kept an eye on things here, for reasons other than Aria's flight. Marina?

Aria turns to me, ghostly pale all of a sudden.

"What is it? Nausea? We can eat something now."

"I'm not sure I feel like it," she says. "That...that was Victor."

Okay. That's definitely bad news. I thought Bellini might have a few men in the area, but I didn't expect him to send his Russian asset.

"Should we get off the train?" Aria asks, anxiously.

I have to think for a moment. They might have figured out that Aria is looking for her mother. Will they assume we're trying to outsmart them by going on an international train and then change? It's a risk to assume anything, but I decide we stick to the plan.

"There's no way they know we'll change trains in Bologna. No, stick to the plan. Then it's all the way to Munich, one night, and we go to Hamburg from there."

Part of me, delusional maybe, still thinks we could maybe catch a flight to Dublin and go back to the cottage, me, anyway. It must be the lack of sleep that makes me think Aria might want to stay...I shake my head as if to ward off the thoughts. We still have a long way to go.

She leans back in her seat, her expression unreadable.

"Hey, don't worry. We made it."

"For now. And I still don't know what happened to Mom."

"Well, you know that she came here freely, and she intended to leave your father. I think Emilia told us the truth. She doesn't know more. Her parents might, but that's something to figure out another time."

"I know we couldn't stay, with Victor and Dad's people here." She sighs. "I don't know what I was expecting. Maybe I should leave it alone. People being threatened and—I don't know what Dad wants from me! He surely didn't care much when I was back home."

I don't voice what's on my mind. It's likely the same thing men like him always want—complete power over others, and especially the women in their lives. Marina. Aria.

I need to find a way to make Rory understand that he's associating with the wrong people. He might have been weakened after Tommy's death, and what happened with Courtney, but he's not without choices. He made peace with the Carusos. I'm not sure Sienna feels especially obliged to me, but she might be willing to help, make him see that Aria can't go home. Not to that.

"Maybe I should call him. Apologize. Maybe it's safer for everyone. Mom, if she's still out there. You."

"No!" The word comes out sharper than intended, and she winces. "Aria, you can't go back. Victor Orlov is not a good guy. Even if he was, you don't want to marry him."

*Please say you don't.*

She looks uncertain. "Of course I don't, but you don't understand—"

"I understand enough. Your father has been telling you all your life how you're obliged to the family and its legacy, and how it's necessary for you to marry a man in order to protect it. That's a lie. Any family that forces someone into an abusive relationship is worthless."

Maybe I'm bitter. It's not that my parents cared so much about a delusion of legacy, but they sure didn't protect me. Not like Rory and Ciara did. There's a reason why I toed the line with them, cut them more slack than others. Otherwise, they'd be in prison now.

Yes, I definitely think Sienna would understand. Can't live with them, can't live without them. But there's a world between Rory Flynn and Antonio Bellini—he just has to understand it.

She's quiet after that, because she knows I'm right. It's a lot to take in. Maybe until now, she had been telling herself that there was a way back, that her father would be happy and change if she could bring her mother home. The evidence suggests something else.

There's a stop. People get off and on, but no one is paying attention to us. When the conductor comes by, I buy another ticket, this time with my credit card. They found us in Rome.

Let them think we're going a different route, hopefully send them on a wild goose chase.

The stop in Bologna passes without incident. We find our connection, and once we're on the way, I buy us some coffee from the service person, and we finally have our breakfast. Aria is still silent.

I can't stand it any longer. "Look, I'm not sorry for what I said. It's the truth. I know it hurt you, and for that, I am sorry."

"I know. It's just that—" She doesn't finish her sentence.

"It's a lot. I get it." When I left the Flynns, it was different. I knew they weren't pleased, but at the same time, I knew they wouldn't come after me. Sure, they would have liked me to marry their son, but my situation differed greatly from Aria's. There was a time when I had been interested, and Rory and Ciara knew it. They took me in when I had nowhere to go, gave me a well-paying job, and for the most part, they respected me and my contributions.

Until Hollis.

Strange to think that I was younger than Aria is now when I started working for them.

I put away the wrapping paper from the pastries and hold out a water bottle to her. She takes a sip and gives it back to me.

"Do you want another coffee? The dining car isn't far."

"Later maybe."

"Okay."

I want to make things better for her. I want to come clean, and there's a whole host of other things I want to do with her, but I'm aware that none of it can happen in the immediate future.

"Wake me if you need anything," I say and lean back. I close my eyes, and it's not long until the motion of the train puts me to sleep.

Aria wakes me gently when the controller arrives to check our ticket, the one we paid cash and that will get us all the way to Munich now. With each passing stop, I feel a little less anxious, or maybe it was just the lack of sleep.

I haven't done a cross-Europe trip in a while, but in many ways, this is not so different from working for the Flynns. Be one step ahead of the enemy.

And I know it in my heart, that if Rory and Tommy hadn't insisted Hollis go with him that night, Tommy would still be alive. *You trusting fool*, I think. I still miss him, and it's a tad awkward that likely, the same goes for Courtney. But she's taken her life back, and I'm about to do the same. I'll do better this time. A lot depends on it, for me, for Aria.

# Chapter Twelve

## Aria

I guess it's true that I'm grieving. The idea of a family I never had, Mom and Dad being happy and in love. Saoirse is right—he likely never gave a damn about her or me. Where that ultimately leaves me, I have no idea. On a train to Munich, for now. I am tired too, almost nodded off a few times, though I definitely slept more last night than she did, and so I secretly enjoyed watching over her, the mysterious woman who has gotten me out of a tricky situation more than once in the past couple of days.

I shudder at the memory of Victor standing on that platform. I can no longer hide from the truth, that part, anyway, because I might never know if Mom made it out, if she found the life she was hoping for. Without me.

I sit up straighter, forcing the thoughts aside. We have to focus on the immediate. I trust Saoirse to assess our situation. She has definitely done something like this before.

I'll leave things to her for the moment. I made it here. I can make it further.

"Can we have lunch in the dining car?" I ask. "I mean, if the cash situation allows it."

A smile softens her features. "I think we can afford it. Let's take our backpacks with us."

Right. Miraculously I had managed to hold on to the Gucci bag throughout my turbulent escape, only to have her tell me I had to leave it behind.

I get it. With our hair tucked underneath baseball caps and Saoirse's tourist outfits, we were able to get away unnoticed. I still have my passport. Some money. My toothbrush and a few toiletries. I can make do until we come to a place where we can stay for a while.

We. The thought makes me smile too. Nothing is ever completely hopeless. I remember it now, how Mom used to say it. Little did I know that she probably needed to convince herself, but I get it now. I can make it through this, build a life away from the name that has given me nothing but fear and pressure.

---

The restaurant on the train isn't cheap, for our circumstances anyway, though I remember, with a hint of guilt, that I used to spend this and more on lunch without thinking. Away from it all, I can now see it clearly, what happened, what Dad did to make me believe this was all normal while he was setting me up.

The train has stopped multiple times, and nothing bad has happened. The further we get away, the more I can breathe. I'm enjoying this lunch with a beautiful woman by my side, even though she likely wouldn't be here if I wasn't in this particular kind of trouble. We're having pasta with a glass of wine, a little ironic, because I would have liked to enjoy all of it in a nice taverna. But I'm starting to think that I might return. This is only the beginning of the journey. For Saoirse and I.

She gives me a smile that makes me feel like we're co-conspirators, and I'm picturing what might develop once we're in Munich. Maybe, Saoirse, too, can relax a little and enjoy a time-out. Maybe...

But we're not there yet. I marvel at the fact that we're both here, our evolution from her being barely more than an image on my mind—a dream, that part is still weird—then a suspicion. I still want to know the truth, but I might have to accept that it comes with more detours than I ever imagined. Not all of them unpleasant.

"What are you thinking?" she asks. Sleeping has done her some good, I think. Some of the wariness is gone from her gaze, the curves of her shoulders more relaxed. Her attention is entirely focused on me, and I'm not sure I've ever felt like this. I shiver with something akin to delight.

"I'm glad," I admit. "To be here. A little proud of myself, both of us, actually. And...if I haven't said it often enough, thank you."

"You're welcome."

"No, I mean for listening to me. People around me kept telling me how fortunate I was, and when I first got on that plane...I was relieved, but also wondering if I was about to make an even bigger mess of things. If it was ridiculous to be this afraid of everything."

"Well, Orlov came all the way to Rome," she reminds me. The tone of her voice makes me shiver too, though in an entirely different way. It's crazy. She doesn't know me, not really, yet I believe her when she says that she'll protect me. There's something absolute in that, and, given my upbringing, it should maybe frighten me, but it doesn't. She's the polar opposite of Victor and the men working for Dad.

"He did."

All the possible implications hang in the air for a few seconds, the fact that he came with armed men, tried several times to

71

get to us even after she had arranged the safehouse. I push the thought of him aside.

"So, Saoirse...What do you do when you don't save damsels in distress?"

Saoirse laughs, and somehow that sound does things to me too. Not like anyone could blame me. The months prior to my escape I was extra careful. I haven't been with anyone in over six months. Now my plans have been derailed slightly, I've escaped the threat of abduction and likely, bodily harm, and I'm tired and in the company of a beautiful, badass woman. How can I not...

"You're hardly a damsel," she says. "And it probably sounds bad, but I'm between things at the moment."

"Are you? What about that friend?"

"Well, that's why I'm between things. He thought you could use some help, which apparently was true. But for the moment, I think it's safer when it's just the two of us."

"Who is he?"

Her expression becomes guarded. "Someone I used to work for. I'm sorry I can't tell you more at this time, though I will once I've cleared up a few things. Can you trust me until then?"

"It's not like I have a choice," is the first thing that comes to mind and over my lips. "But yes. I think your record so far speaks for itself. If you wanted to take me back home...you've had plenty of opportunities so far."

"I wouldn't," she says, and that, too, sounds final. "I'm tired of men like him."

She doesn't elaborate if she means Victor, Dad, or that mysterious "friend" of hers. I remain curious. About all the people who have a more or less selfish interest in designing my future.

About Saoirse.

"Dessert?" she asks.

"Oh yes. Please."

Given our record, it's not so sure when we'll have the chance next.

"I hope the cash doesn't run out altogether before this is over," I muse.

"Why?"

"Because a relaxing vacation would be nice, wouldn't it?"

"Yeah," she admits with a wistful smile. "I do know just the spot."

Saoirse flexes her fingers a little, unrelated to anything maybe, but it makes me shift in my seat. I see the hint of amusement. She misses nothing.

# Chapter Thirteen

## Saoirse

At this point, the one-bed option isn't just a trope, it's a necessity for us to save time and money, and to make sure we can leave quickly if the need arises. Our hotel room in Munich is tiny, and I can't help the smirk when I see Aria's eyes widen. Despite all we, that she went through already.

"We should take a quick shower and sleep. Train's early tomorrow."

"Yeah, what else is new?" She yawns.

I lay a hand on her shoulder. "Aria, Hamburg is two hours from Rome by plane. If anything came up regarding your mother, and we knew it was safe to go back, we would. For now, it would help to lay low. Victor can't hunt you forever."

I almost regret my words when I feel her tremble under my hand, but it's the truth. That's what it is to him. People like him. God, I'm still mad at Rory for his sins of omission regarding Courtney Flynn, and he's by far not the worst.

Or is he?

I have to find out how much he knew prior to asking me for that favor. Yes, I told Aria something else, but going forward, we need to know what we're dealing with.

"I guess I better take that shower."

"Yes."

When she opens the door to the bathroom, I have to step back to make room. When she's inside, I suppress a sigh as I look around. It's certainly nothing like the Flynns' mansion, or the cottage. The cottage...I fell in love with it the moment I walked through the door. Kind of like when I first laid eyes on Aria. I had hoped my life would be a little less complicated once I left the Flynns, but it doesn't look like it's going to happen.

Ironically, it's still all dangerous assignments and unfulfilled desires, Saoirse Reilly at your service. I almost laugh at that. Nerves.

There are heavy footsteps outside in the hallway, laughter. I tense, but the guests continue to walk, and now I hear the happy squeal of a child and exhale. Nothing is going to stop us. We'll get to Hamburg, stay for a few days, and I'll call in every possible favor to inquire about Marina Bellini, born Cacciatore.

Aria doesn't have any interest in going back to the States at this moment, and I allow myself the fleeting fantasy that she might want to come to Ireland with me. Maybe there was more to the cliché I've been scoffing at, people feeling called to a land they've never visited before. It could be home, for both of us.

Yeah.

Right.

Nothing complicated about that.

Aria comes out of the bathroom wrapped in only a towel. She holds my gaze, well aware that I can't look away, her long dark hair still damp and curling, the fabric revealing the swell of her breasts, and her legs up to mid-thigh. If this is part of the cliché, she sure knows how to work it. It's not that I feel like I owe anyone at this point. It's not about the ethics of getting involved with a client. I'm afraid that too many emotions, too little distance, could lead to the same result as the last time I was in charge, and I could never forgive myself.

Spooked, I wordlessly pick up my clothes and head into the miniscule bathroom where I get ready quickly, cursing when I bang my elbow in the shower stall. It's only for a few hours. It will do.

Tomorrow, we'll be in Hamburg in slightly better accommodations. I chose this place because it's close to the train station. Before I head back into the room, I look at my phone that is once again blowing up with messages from Rory.

*What does Bellini have on you? Get in touch with Sienna if necessary. Aria isn't coming back,* I type, then I turn it off.

Aria pretends to be asleep, which is just fine with me. I climb into the double bed and turn my back to her, willing myself to fall asleep quickly, not be distracted by the scent of the hotel shampoo and shower gel that somehow smells delicious on her. If nothing out of the ordinary happens, we can have breakfast downstairs after checking out, then go right to the central station a couple of minutes away.

I am excited, to be honest. Maybe I, too, am feeling for the first time what it's like to be free.

Despite the constant pressure, I fall into a surprisingly deep and restful sleep, only interrupted by what I think is a dream at first, Aria's arms coming around me, her lips brushing my neck as her naked body presses against me. It's such a magnificent feeling I can't help leaning into dream Aria, the sensations enough to make me moan. And that makes it extremely real all of a sudden, the sound, Aria's hands on my body, under my shirt, fingers sneaking past the waistband of my boxers.

Not a dream. She's right here in bed with me, and gloriously naked all right. I gasp, and when I turn around, there's a smile on her face. Knowing. A bit relieved, too. I feel horrible about having to kill the mood.

"Aria, what are you doing?"

"What do you think it is I'm doing? Look, I know what you're going to say, but I...I've been really scared." She shakes her head. "No, that didn't come out right. It's not because I'm scared—which I am, but that's not the point." We stare at each other in a silent standoff.

"You don't know what I was going to say." My argument is weak, and I'm aware of it. My face is still warm, and the heat is quickly traveling to other places. It shows in my voice.

"Don't you want this? Me?" Aria is all but holding her breath waiting for the answer she already knows. I want her so much, especially since that kiss, that I can barely control myself around her. It's scary for many reasons. Giving up control is uncomfortable. It could be fatal.

Reasons? Excuses, because I'm the one who's afraid?

I reach out, nearly gasp again when my fingers encounter warm skin.

Any point I might have wanted to make is vanishing rapidly.

"What do you think?" I ask. We kiss again, and I know I'm going to give in this time, no matter what. We don't know how much time we have. I'm scared all right, but I also don't want to live with the regret of asking myself what if.

I kiss her deeply, thrilled by her nakedness, frustrated with the last pieces of clothing between us. I'm out of them before Aria has the time to help me with the task, and then I pull her to me, maintaining that last bit of control, or trying to.

She's a lot less shy now, following me eagerly, opening to my questing fingers, her sounds of approval unmistakable.

Like I said—I haven't been with many women. Fortunately, those few count. They were gentle, encouraging.

I don't have to worry. If anything, Aria might be a bit too enthusiastic, and I put a finger to her lips.

"I'm not sure how thin the walls are in this place," I say.

Even our shared laughter is tinged with arousal. We can't ever come back from this. My mind is overflowing with everything I want to do to her, though she seems happy with what I'm coming up with. I push the cover aside as a memory is coming back to me.

Don't worry about it too much. Try not to be in your head. It's not that complicated. It wasn't. It isn't. Aria stiffens against me, lying still in my arms for a little while. Seconds, minutes? I find myself on my back, her mouth exploring me, my breasts, my stomach, a heated path downwards until I have to bite my lip to stay silent.

I remember that glorious sensation as well.

I didn't think it would happen in a small, cheap hotel room in Munich, with a rebelling mafia princess, but here we are. I close my eyes and let myself go. For these precious seconds, she's keeping me completely safe.

——⁓——

We don't talk much after that, simply because there's nothing much to say we can't express with gestures, touches, kisses. We still have to find some sleep, get up early today, head out. Much of the next few days, let alone weeks, is still uncertain, but at least we don't have to wonder any longer. Aria smiles against my chest as I'm stroking her hair, and I wonder if she had that in mind when she toasted to me in that restaurant. Not that it matters. Questions, past regrets.

We have the here and now.

"I don't think I've ever been happy before. Not since Mom went missing, but certainly not as an adult."

It would be sad, maybe, if I couldn't relate so much, if we hadn't had this chance. Because I hear what she says between the lines. Maybe someday, I'll tell her about my family. About Rory, and all the rest of it.

Happy for now is already so much more than I imagined, and I think the same goes for her.

I hold her tighter, again making the point without words.

---

Our short stay here is definitely less frantic. Keeping an eye on the clock, we have breakfast in the small, traditionally furnished breakfast room.

"I had one of those when I first arrived here," Aria says as she picks a pretzel from the buffet. "Wow, was I ever mistaken about how my time here was going to go."

"Well, I hope not all of it was bad," I say, teasing her as I make my own choices.

"Some parts were pretty amazing. I love that you're blushing."

I make a face. Nothing I can do against genetics.

"It's warm in here," I say. "Come on, let's eat."

A friendly hotel employee brings a thermal carafe with fresh, strong coffee to the table. Aria and I share a look. Exactly what we needed.

I still have to call Rory, not just because I want to make my stance clear, but because he's the only one who can tell me what Bellini is up to.

Later, when we're halfway to Hamburg and everything is quiet during a longer stretch without stops, I excuse myself to go to the restroom. It's a bit shaky, and I'm not sure about the cell phone reception, but it will have to do.

"Saoirse, what the hell?" he thunders. "You have to come in at once. And bring Aria, wherever you're keeping her. Antonio says he'll make sure there will be an international warrant out for your arrest! You think I'll be able to protect you then? Or that Sienna, or your FBI friend will? What the hell were you thinking?"

"She's not my FBI friend," I say, as if my relationship with Ryan Farmer matters at all. "Rory, tell me what's going on. If Aria is in danger from anyone, it's her father, and Orlov."

His only answer is a heavy sigh. The signal is fading, and I'm afraid I'm going to lose him.

"Don't you remember what all the lies have cost us in the past?"

"I remember very well, Saoirse. And I'll regret it for the rest of my life that I sent Hollis with him that night instead of you. I just thought...It doesn't matter anymore."

"Courtney barely survived. Armed men came after Aria in Rome. Those weren't Bellini's business partners. She recognized Orlov."

"I couldn't hold them back. They weren't sure you were up for the job. You never touched the money."

"No, and I have no intention of doing so. Rory, I need you to promise me that you didn't give up our location. Neither Bellini nor Orlov is safe for her."

"And you can tell?" I don't even think he's questioning my assessment. He's bitter and depressed about his choices, some of which I can understand. It's no excuse.

"I'm not bringing her back. And I'll keep them away from her with everything I've got. I'm serious."

"You always were."

Oh, no, now is not the time to get nostalgic about the past.

"Was I right? Does he have something on you?"

"I know what it's like to lose a child," he replies, an air of indignation to his tone.

"Does he?" I ask, sharper this time.

"It's not what you think. I told you, we need strong alliances."

"And it was wise to repair the one you once had with the Carusos, even though your common ground was that you didn't give a damn about Tommy's wife."

"Saoirse, that's enough."

"No, it's not, not by far. I need you to back out of this and stick with halfway decent partners, because whether that makes sense or not, I still give a damn. And I need you to tell me what Bellini is up to. Now."

The silence makes me fear I've lost the connection, but then he speaks.

"I care about you too. Ciara and I both do, always have. I don't want anything to happen to you, so it would be best if you could let this go. Antonio isn't going to rest. If it's not you, someone else will find Aria."

"Aria will be a prisoner. His, then Orlov's. I won't let that happen."

"Saoirse..."

"Stop. You have a chance here, to do something decent. Take it. If you can't keep me informed, then this will be the last time we speak in a while."

"Saoirse, where are you two going?"

"I can't tell you."

"I'll see what I can find out. But I, too, have a family to think about."

"You know, once upon a time, before Kevin Hollis came along, you treated me like family."

"You still are!"

"Prove it," I say and end the call. I splash cold water on my face and grimace at my mirror image. That could have gone better—or worse. Perspective is everything.

I think that for the time being, we'll be safe on this train, and, for a few days, in Hamburg.

# Chapter Fourteen

## Aria

We buy a bottle of wine at the supermarket, and pizza from a nearby restaurant. For tonight, it's another small room in a hostel, though slightly bigger than Munich, then we will find something more...Well, not actually permanent. Somewhere we can do laundry, cook, and still be under the radar.

I'm not kidding myself. Saoirse is a secretive woman. Everything I hated at home? With her, it only adds a layer of mystery and intrigue, because unlike the people I've been around, she's not scheming or cruel. I know she hasn't told me everything, and I know better than to ask about why she's been pensive for the past hour. Her face lights up once we've made it to our room. Just the two of us. I could get used to that, making love in the late afternoon with the curtains drawn, before we heat up the pizza in the shared kitchen.

I know what it's like to have one's boundaries disrespected, so I vow to honor hers. She'll talk to me when she's ready. Meanwhile, I'm happy to be close to her, sharing another meal in relative safety. I know she's been reaching out to contacts of hers to inquire about Mom. I have to be patient.

"Do you think it's safe to go in the city for a bit? Not now," I clarify. "In the next few days. I'd love a few more clothes, and a few books."

"Books?" she asks as if that's a surprise.

"Hey, I happen to read. There were times in my life when books were all I had. The adventures of girls whose parents weren't part of...well. I just want a couple. I still have cash too, and a few pre-paid cards."

"I think that's fine. Between here and the next safehouse, we'll make time. I'm going to meet with someone...If she can't tell me more about your mom, I don't think anyone can."

"Oh. Okay. Can I meet her too?"

I expect a flat-out no. Instead, Saoirse shrugs. "If she's okay with it, I don't see why not." My surprise must have shown, because she adds, "I told you, I was going to share when I could. But this is up to her."

"I understand."

That's not really the truth, but I see it as a step forward. I pour us some more wine and take another piece of pizza. "Let's watch some TV, okay?"

I find a channel with international news, almost expecting to see a familiar face. Nothing about the incident...incidents in Rome though. I change the channel again, and we try to figure out the plot of a German movie. For this evening, we're silly and happy, cherishing our time together as if nothing else matters.

—ele—

The next day, we buy a few clothes first before we head to a bookstore. I'm browsing the selections for mysteries, fondly reminiscing the way Saoirse and I started this morning, when Dad calls me.

Saoirse is standing at the bestsellers table, a few feet away out of earshot. As if I could ever pretend this other reality didn't exist...She didn't finish her glass last night, pays attention to everything and everyone. She never rests, and as much as it's a relief, it's also a reminder that it's not yet the time to let our guards down completely.

But that phone. It can't ring. No one's supposed to have this number. I smile and point to the restroom, and she's leaving her place, walking toward me. So, she'll wait outside the door. Okay. I hurry up, lock myself in a stall and stare at the number. It can't be.

My heart is hammering, but all of a sudden, I feel daring. With Saoirse by my side, what do I have to fear? We'll be gone soon anyway, and while Dad might have a cop or two in his pocket, he doesn't have the technology to trace me. He's not a supervillain, just...I'll save that for later. Acknowledging that your father is a criminal isn't easy even when you're about to cut all ties. It makes you wonder if there's something inevitable in your DNA. After all, I've been traveling with two passports.

"Hello, Aria," he says. "I was wondering when you'd check in with me. How's London?"

My bravery doesn't last long. I can barely get the words out. Seeing Victor on that platform, starting to understand what it all means, I'm terrified. But I need him to understand something too.

"We were a bit worried about you. When are you coming home?"

"Dad, there's been a slight change of plans."

"What change?" he asks, and I picture him frowning. However, until this moment, his tone has been cordial, kind even. I lost the ability to trust it.

"I like it here. I'm not coming back."

He knows I never went to London.

"What makes you say that? You have your whole life waiting for you here."

I want to ask him about Mom, but I can't. I can't physically force out the words, because I'm scared of what I might hear. Angry and frustrated about what lies he might tell me. Again.

"The life you planned for me. I don't want any of it. I don't want to marry Victor."

"Victor?" He bursts out laughing. Why didn't I realize sooner that he's never taken me seriously? Maybe, because it wasn't safe before I had a plan. "But that was a joke! You marry whoever you want when the time is right. Of course, I will personally vet the man. You understand that we can't hand over the family fortune to just anyone."

"Right." This likely isn't the right moment to come out to him either. Not that I feel obliged, not anymore. "I saw him. On a train platform."

Dad isn't denying the charges.

"There was never a business partner who threatened you, was there? You made it all up and then hired someone to track me down..."

"Aria, please, don't be hysterical. I need you to calm down. Victor never had anything but your best interests in mind, otherwise he would have paid dearly, I can promise you that."

"He tried to kiss me against my will."

"And he apologized, didn't he? Look, I don't know what you have against him, but we had to take precautions. There are many people out there who want to get to me through you. The more you know, the more dangerous it could be for you. Do you think I wanted to keep you behind closed doors for most of your life? I need you here at home. It's not a good time for you to be childish."

"Goodbye, Dad," I say, put the phone in my pocket and open the door of the stall. Saoirse is right there, her expression emotionless.

"You got the books you wanted?" she asks. "Let's go have a coffee somewhere."

I'm scared to ask how much she has overheard, but the tone of her voice reveals it: Everything.

"Why are you so angry with me? He called me," I say, hurrying after her. "I told him I wouldn't come back."

"You should have gotten rid of that phone the moment you saw it was him," she says. "I think it's all a lot of bluster, so we'll have time for that coffee. Continue as planned. We're leaving the hotel today."

I can feel myself blanch.

"Today? You don't think...?"

"I'm not sure what I think," she admits. "But we'll get to the bottom of it."

Somehow, I still think she's angry at me, and I'm not sure if she means it as a promise or a threat.

How did my father get this number?

I can't be this wrong about her, can I?

―――

I'm a bit relieved after that coffee, feeling less silly with my bags of purchases. No, it wasn't a good idea to answer that phone. It's not likely that he can trace it, but yes, the fact that he has that number is disconcerting.

Saoirse is still in hypervigilant mode.

"I promised you I'll meet with my contact about your mom. I don't know that we can stay here longer."

"I'm sorry. But I'm pretty sure he was fishing...I didn't tell him where we were. You believe me, right?"

Saoirse lets out a sigh. "Yes. I believe you. But if you want me to protect you, I need you to be honest with me, okay? We'll ditch the phone. We can get you a new one later. And no more going off on your own."

"Which, obviously, goes only one way."

Why do I have to challenge her? It's not like I have any other ally. That, and I don't want to alienate her, because of what? Stupid habit? I still can't imagine he's that bad? I only have to remember what he said about the man I was going to marry. I heard everything between the lines I needed to. He'll never accept me the way I am.

"I am so sorry," I say again. "Where will we go?"

She looks like she's contemplating that. "I could tell you where I'd like to go, but we can't be sure it's safe. I do have many more contacts in the States."

"No way. Dad would find me easily."

"He found you here, didn't he?" Saoirse shakes her head, as frustrated as I am. "I don't want to fight with you, Aria. You knew that this was risky."

"I know. It's just...I'm going back and forth. I've been living in that house for all my life. He's been distant, and I hated being watched all of the time. For all I know he might have killed my mother." Tears fill my eyes. I don't want this, to spoil everything, but I'm at my wit's end. I don't know how much longer I can cope with all this new information, and yet, still, the lack of information, truth, that I need. "I know he's not a good guy. It's silly, but maybe I thought—"

"That he might have changed?" she asks softly.

"It's ridiculous, really. He told me I could marry whoever I wanted to, after he vetted him."

"It's human. I understand."

"Do you? Your father is also a clever criminal who manipulates everyone around him?"

"I don't know about clever," she says, pensive again. "Not a good guy either. But I understand about hoping that someone deserves your trust and being disappointed."

"Well, I don't ever want to disappoint you. Do we really have to leave?"

"Just to go to the safehouse a bit earlier. That should do it."

However, when we get to the hostel, we don't pack right away. I can still taste the sugary treat we've shared, on her lips. It's a rush, dangerous maybe but inevitable, and maybe she wants to remind me why I'm here, not that I need prompting. Now that it's no longer fantasy, her touch makes my knees weak, knowing the pleasure that's coming my way. I know Saoirse has been conflicted about this, us, but she's no longer hesitant. This time, we don't even bother getting naked, when pushing fabric aside works just fine.

I meant what I said: I will never disappoint her again.

———ele———

We quietly pack up our belongings, including my books and the new clothes, and head out. A part of me can't help feeling like I've betrayed her, but Saoirse is back to her old self. I decide we're going to leave it at that. It must have been an unlucky coincidence, that Victor and Dad somehow found this number.

That doesn't mean they know where we went, because Dad was still fishing. It will be all right. It's still only a little over a week since I left. He and Victor will move on to bigger things once they realize I'm not planning on going to the police. That would be ridiculous anyway, because I have nothing to give them, no proof that the men that came after me the first time were really related to him.

Still, I've adopted some of the same habits. We leave a bag of clothing in a donation bin and take a train across the city where we settle into the new place, a furnished apartment more spacious than the recent hotel rooms.

"You are really good at your job," I say, hoping it comes across as intended.

Saoirse draws me into a hug, holding on tightly before she steps back.

"Thank you. I talked to Willow. She doesn't mind if you come with me to the meeting. They have their own security, so you can be certain it's safe."

I must admit it, I'm curious. Who is this woman and why would she know about my mother?

"They happen to be in Hamburg at this moment, and they thought it would be safer to meet in person." When I don't react right away, she adds, "I trust them. You don't have to be afraid."

It's all still chaos in my mind, but if Saoirse says it's okay, I'm sure it is. Unlike Dad, she has little reason to lie to me. And it's ridiculous to think that she'd draw this out, us, traveling all over Europe...I can't believe there's still the flicker of a thought after everything we've shared, but I'm certain that if she was working for Dad, I'd have been in that car with those men, probably about to attend a wedding against my will.

"I trust you," I say, and kiss her like a person who's drowning. Maybe that's who I've been, and she has done an excellent job pulling me out every time.

# Chapter Fifteen

## Saoirse

I am lucky to have cultivated a network over time. Some of it, I owe to my association to the Flynn family. Other parts, I achieved through sheer perseverance, paying attention, taking the right steps at the right time. Willow is a bit of both. We went to college together, Tommy, me, Willow and her then-boyfriend.

A lot has changed for all of us.

"I'm sorry about Tommy," she says, because it's the first time we meet in person since it happened. I shrug, aware of Aria's gaze that is as kind as it's curious, and we move on. Accompanying Willow is a tall brunette, her wife I hadn't met before. Introductions are made, and I thank them for meeting with us.

"It's no problem. We love a good mystery."

The other woman nudges her gently, a hint of amusement to her expression.

Aria isn't offended though.

"Well, you got one on your hands," she says as we sit around the rather private table. Precautions have been made. We wouldn't be here otherwise. "I understand you've looking into my mother's disappearance."

"We have, as best as we could," Willow says with a nod to me. "And let me tell you, we are good at this, so if there's anything to find, we usually do. You already know that your mother asked her friends for help fourteen years ago, and they've been sort of on the run ever since."

"So, she did get away?" Aria asks with a frown.

"Back then, definitely. The bad news is, we don't have anything more recent than about five months ago."

"Five months!" Aria exclaims, then lowers her voice as the server arrives with drinks and appetizer plates.

"Don't worry," Kat, Willow's wife, says. "Everyone and everything here are vetted. Now, what Willow means to say…"

Willow lays an envelope in front of us. "This woman was working in a hotel in Mexico five months ago. We checked. She's not there anymore, and there's been no trace of her ever since. She used the name Maria Cacciatore."

Maria, which might be short for Marina. It also could combine Marina and Aria, I muse, and seeing the excited glow on Aria's cheeks, I wonder if she's thinking the same thing.

"That's my mom's maiden name," she says as she opens the envelope and takes out the photos. "Mexico?"

"That doesn't mean she's still there. In fact, we couldn't find any record since she left that employment."

What the hell happened five months ago? Aria was already planning her trip. Were they on to her? Her mother?

"I was way behind then. She wasn't in Rome after all."

"She stayed in Italy for a few years, left about two years ago."

I exchange a look with Aria, who is shaking her head, obviously still processing all that new information. "It's amazing. She's still alive…" I can see something else in her gaze. The timeframe means nothing to me, but I assume it does to her. Aria's next words prove me right.

"Victor has been working for Dad longer than that, but it was around that time that the marriage jokes started. You've got to be kidding me. He wants to punish me for what she did? She was able escape again, so he's going to lock me up forever?"

I wouldn't put that kind of thinking past Bellini, but I'm almost certain that there's more to the story.

"Do you have any idea how much your mother knew about the daily operations?"

Willow's question is diplomatic, her tone warm and kind. We are on to something. What if Bellini found his missing wife, but she escaped again, and he moved on to Plan B?

But what's the incentive here—simply having the upper hand, establishing himself as a man who has his house in order? There's still a missing piece.

"I don't know. I've never been privy to anything illegal, though I've heard the general accusations. That there's drug money involved, money laundering, and since Victor came along, well, you can guess."

"Murder?"

Aria flinches, and I cast a sharp glance at Kat who looks back at me, unimpressed.

"It would help if you could give the authorities something eventually. They might be interested in what happened to your mother as well. She might be an important witness."

Sure, but did she want to be? Would it be safe for her to reemerge and testify against her husband? We've been on a wild race through Europe which would suggest otherwise. It's still hard to assess how far Bellini's network really goes. Knowing about his motivations would help. He might have focused his efforts simply on his family. It takes resources, but not as many if his criminal empire really extended all over Europe and North America.

I doubt it. After my years up close with the Flynns and, by proxy, some of their partners, I know not to underestimate them. I also know a lot of it is bluster and ego, all of which leads to mistakes eventually. Foot soldiers get caught, and eventually the authorities get to go up the chain.

Rory needs to get a grip and come clean.

"I wouldn't know any of it, I'm sorry." There's an urgency to Aria's tone. She wants us to believe it, me, the women who have just provided her with a lifeline. To be honest, I didn't think they'd get that far.

"Did your parents ever tell you about how they met?" Willow again.

"What does that have to do with anything?" Aria sounds irritated, and I can't blame her.

The server brings another round of drinks, and the main course. We eat and drink in silence, the question lingering in the air. Is there really a need to go back further? On the other hand, I don't think Willow would ask this question on a whim. Maybe she did find the missing piece.

"Fourteen years is a long time to hold a grudge. I'm just trying to get the whole picture. Clearly, your mother attempted to stay hidden. I don't think the timeline is a coincidence. Any of it."

"Well, thank you for all of your work. I really appreciate it. That might be all there is."

"Feel free to read my report. If there's anything that stands out, anything you can remember that helps, Saoirse can get back to me."

Under the table, I lay a hand on Aria's knee, to reassure her. She exhales, gives me a grateful smile.

"I think I have to go to the bathroom."

"I'll go with you."

"Saoirse."

Aria is already halfway to the restroom, and I don't hide my irritation as I turn to Willow. Kat has gotten up as well and follows Aria.

"They'll be okay for a while," Willow says. "Please, sit. We don't have a lot of time."

"What is this?"

I'm too intrigued though. This is all beyond curious.

"I don't have proof. It's all rumors as of now, but there was an accident when Aria was little. Some say Bellini attempted to kill his wife."

"What?" I cast a quick glance at the restroom door, but it remains closed. "I don't know. He had the means to do it. Why give up and give her enough time to escape?"

"I don't know yet, but the guy had some sort of long-term plan. With Marina, with Aria. Word is that since both of them managed to fool him, he's getting angrier by the minute, looking to get back at them...and at everyone who's mocking him."

"He brought that on himself, obviously." The men at the top of organized crime aren't always known for their logic. Don't get me wrong, they are clever when evading capture and any accountability, but they are also quite...emotional. Antiono Bellini, case in point.

"Sure. But there's something else." So, she noticed it too. "He could just take care of this quietly, instead of creating such a spectacle. There's a lot of hate in all this. Hunting down your wife and daughter." She shudders a little. "Handing Aria over to Orlov. The guy is rumored to have been a secret agent for his home country."

"Yeah, I've heard that."

"He's a big part of why people have been more scared of Bellini in recent years, and for a reason."

"What does Bellini have to gain from Aria marrying Victor, other than getting the last word?" I wonder out loud. "Victor was never going to let her have a say in the business. In fact, I don't think he's qualified at all. He's not even a reliable ally to Bellini."

"Bellini used him for the dirty jobs, now he has a lot on him, I assume. Basically, he has a huge chip on his shoulder about Marina, and now Aria, and everyone else is just a pawn in the game, even Orlov."

That sounds...real, but still too vague.

"Orlov has his own agenda, though. Get his hands on the business and Aria. Maybe he even thinks he can take out Bellini along the way."

"You could be right. This is a pretty volatile situation and has been for a while. Aria is lucky to have you."

I shrug, my face heating. I doubt that it's a compliment I deserve.

"Lucky is right. I was there at the right time."

Willow holds my gaze, and for a moment I'm worried she knows the rest of it, but Aria and Kat return to the table before she can say anything.

"Okay, who's ready for dessert?" she asks instead, smiling.

Everything is all right, at least for the moment. We're lucky to have friends in important places, though the news is disconcerting.

Bellini is stinking rich. What would he have to gain from Marina's and Aria's deaths?

⁓

After dinner, Willow's driver brings us back to the safehouse, where we lock all entrances with the smart software, each of our minds laden with thoughts.

"I'm glad it looks like your mom is alive," I finally break the silence.

Aria offers a small smile. "Yes, me too. What did you and Willow talk about?"

"Just catching up. We went to college together, you know."

"I do now. Wow, this is...It's good and terribly bad at the same time. I doubt I'll get to have a happy reunion anytime soon, even if Mom wanted that. Is there really nothing we can do, other than hide out and take multiple eight-hour train rides?"

"We'll stay here for now," I promise her and draw her close. I can tell from the way she leans into my embrace how tired she is. We won't run forever. That's not the job. That's not the promise I made to her, to myself.

She and I will be home someday, hopefully together.

Tonight, we simply hold each other close, and it's a small but profound glimpse at that future.

I had that fleeting moment of peace.

I want more of it. With her.

# Chapter Sixteen

## Aria

I can't be too sure of anything, except Saoirse's friends have a lot of strange questions, and the most amazing news of all, Mom is likely alive and hiding out somewhere, like we are. Mexico. Maybe another country altogether. What if there's a way that we could be in each other's lives, far away—or at least, far enough—from Dad's war and power games?

I don't understand why he can't just let us go. I strongly suspect that Mom knows as little as I do. He has lawyers who would discredit us in a heartbeat if we tried to implicate him.

That's not my job anyway, I think, stubbornly clinging to that dream, and to Saoirse.

I can't help laughing, and that seems to alarm her.

"What's the matter?"

"It's…" All of a sudden, I can't stop. "It's ridiculous. This is a movie, not anyone's real life. Dad isn't some sort of criminal mastermind, is he? His influence is not infinite." I sit up against the headboard, trying to catch my breath. How unreal is this? I'm in Hamburg, in Germany, with a woman I met only days ago. Then again, being under constant surveillance, what used to be my life, feels equally unreal. I never want to go back to that.

The fact that Dad was able to sustain this impossible situation for so long, what does it mean?

In any case, nothing has happened since the call. Maybe they did lose the trace. Fuck those megalomaniac antics. And fuck Victor.

"Are you okay?" Saoirse asks dryly, though with a hint of concern. "Do you need anything...water?"

"No, thank you." I do my best to voice my thoughts in a calmer manner. "We are okay."

"For now," she reminds me. "We must be patient a little longer. You read all of the report?"

"I did. There are still things that don't make sense to me, but I'm glad—" I halt, because somehow, that word doesn't seem big enough. "I'm so relieved..." It might be the wine we had for dinner, or my overall state, a mix of constant high alert, fear, never mind helpless attraction for this woman. My eyes are welling up.

"I know. This is hopeful. I doubt that they got to her. She's clearly resourceful...like her daughter."

"I was lucky to have resources," I admit. "I don't know how I would have done this without access to money. Dad just trusted that I'd never be able to spend it like this." I let out a heavy sigh. "I always had to be so quick and make up reasons for some purchases that I thought would seem suspicious. I guess I got really good at lying...or they didn't think I had it in me."

"Fools," Saoirse scoffs. "It worked to our advantage, but I knew not to underestimate you when I first saw you."

"I toasted you with that Amaretto," I say wistfully. "Then I got scared, and two minutes later they tried to drag me into that car. What a trip this has been."

"It will get better," she insists, reaching out to touch my arm. I revel in the small gesture that means so much more now. "We'll lay low for a few days, and if nothing happens, we'll decide where to go from here. Willow's people will keep looking. In any case it doesn't look like Marina would go back to Rome, especially if the places she knows are crawling with Bel—your father's men."

"I didn't know what to believe." The loss of touch makes me start shivering. "To be honest, I got scared that they, Victor, might have killed her. I don't care if it's hearsay or rumors. I know he's capable of that. And...I'm so, so sorry for taking that call!"

Fortunately, Saoirse isn't fazed by my rapidly changing moods, because she wraps her arms around me and holds on tightly.

"Family is tricky," she says. "Believe me, I know. And you just got out. It will be all right."

I got out, right. I had been so single-mindedly focused on getting away and to that address in Rome, I might not have considered all that this entails. Dad's reassurances were far from believable. Which means I am cutting all ties with everything I've ever known, finding Mom not a guarantee.

And all of a sudden it feels heavy, more than I've ever imagined. Because it means that I don't know who I really am.

I hope she's right. For the moment, I have no choice other than to believe her.

"Besides," Saoirse says, "You were right, finding that trace of Marina is a big deal. I think we have a reason to celebrate."

# Chapter Seventeen

## Saoirse

I know that despite the good news, Aria is still struggling to come to terms with the ways her life will be forever altered. I can't help feeling hopeful for the first time in a while. Willow's report might be concerning in many ways, but nothing has happened since Bellini's call. Aria and I are on the same page, and I won't raise the idea of going back to the States at the moment.

When I go to the kitchen to prepare the promised celebration, I see that Rory sent an email with an attachment.

*I appreciate you warning me. Sienna and I had a long talk. It's time to step back from Antonio.*

I barely suppress the sigh. Took you long enough. I don't type it, just reply *You're welcome.*

To be honest, I'm surprised he's taking my advice at this point. It's a good development though. I briefly wonder how Courtney feels about this, though I'm sure Sienna will have no trouble drawing boundaries. I also think of perpetually frustrated Ryan Farmer, scowling at how much all of us have gotten away with. Then I take the bottle from the fridge, two glasses, and walk back into the living room.

Everything else can wait.

When I return, Aria's face lights up so spectacularly at the sight of me, I nearly blush again. But I know I've made the right choices.

After a few weeks in that cottage outside of Dublin, I thought peace was a place, somewhere to feel rooted. I'm starting to understand that much more than that, it's a person, *that* person, something I've never experienced before.

Here, Italy, Ireland, or back home, it doesn't matter. It will always be the same person.

---

The next few days pass in blessed quietude, no chases across another major city, no abrupt departure. Rory sends a few more texts. He's being a bit cagey. What I read between the lines is that he's cutting his losses, good for him. I'll do the same. Maybe I will give Agent Farmer a call and a few tips as to where to look next.

For the time being, I'm still cautious. Regardless, we take walks in the neighborhood and visit the local supermarket for food. There's a pub at the end of the street, and we have dinner there one day.

"You know, before I went to Rome, I had been staying in Ireland," I say. The surroundings are making me wistful, and even a little excited about the future. "We could go there someday if you want. Once things are a little less wild."

"I'd love that," she says without hesitation, making my heart flutter.

I can see it so clearly. A part of me is also waiting for the other shoe to drop, and I'm a heartbeat away from blurting out the truth. Secrets were always a big deal in the Flynn house. Even though I trusted Tommy and his parents as much as I trusted anyone at that time, I learned to guard my own. Ironic how Aria and Tommy have quite a bit in common, except they made different choices.

"Then it's a plan," I say.

Easier said than done, because we need to take Orlov out of the equation, at least. It's hard to say how much time and resources Bellini will spend before giving up. Which means he needs to be distracted, be too busy at home to keep chasing after his daughter.

It's all risky and dangerous, but then again, I've never fled from risk. I'll figure it out.

And mingling with those ever-present concerns and questions is a sense of something deep, calm and utterly surprising. Some might even call it love, not that I ever would after such a short time, even with amazing Aria. I can't take my eyes, or my hands off of her, something I prove to her once again when we are back at our temporary home. She is eager and warm underneath me, encouraging me, not quiet now that we are in a real apartment. I don't try to make her, every sound spilling over those beautiful lips pushing me closer to the edge.

I am in love.

I wish I could trick my mind into fully believing that everything will be all right for us, but as I listen to her rapidly beating heart, the lingering air is bittersweet.

---

While Aria is still asleep the next morning, I get back to work, a bit more research on Victor Orlov. I'm sure that the list of crimes he has committed is longer than his short rap sheet, from the time prior to his employment at Bellini's, suggests. Now, he has access to high-priced lawyers and a network that relies heavily on threats to prosecutors and jurors.

Another email from Willow comes in, and when I open that information, my jaw drops. Perhaps I should have seen it before. This might tie the pieces together. It makes more sense now, hunting Marina and Aria. Because he doesn't want Aria to ever find out.

It's definitely not out of loyalty to family that Bellini doesn't want to let go of her, and that he prefers to leave her with as few choices as possible. Even with this new information, it's nauseating to think that he basically adopted Orlov.

I hear sounds from the bedroom and put my phone aside. I'll have to tell her, but not before coffee and breakfast, so I busy myself preparing the latter.

Aria walks inside, stretching with a yawn.

"I slept so well, it's ridiculous," she says.

I force myself to return her smile. "I'd like to think I had something to do with that."

"Oh, you definitely did. First you wore me out, then you kept the nightmares away." She reaches out to touch my hair, sinks her fingers into the auburn strands. "Witchy woman."

"Such a cliché." I have to laugh, though that knowledge weighs on me. "You feel bewitched?"

"In the best possible way." She leans against the counter. "So, what's the plan today? Is it time to take that plane to Dublin yet?"

Oh, how I wish it was. But as much as I'm glad Rory seems to be coming to his senses, I can't be sure about what information he shared with Bellini before. The last thing I want is to lead him and his crown prince to us.

"Not yet. Be a bit more patient, please?"

"Convince me?" she whispers, leaning in to kiss me. I lightly push her back against the counter, allowing the kiss to become deep, messy, urgent. I don't have witchcraft at my disposal, but I've become pretty good at reading her. My lips against her neck, my fingers teasing and slipping beneath the waistband of her PJ shorts, I think we both know breakfast is postponed.

Aria's sweet surrender is everything to me, but when she gets to her knees in a fluid motion, I take a step back.

"Let's eat," I say, the rasp in my voice belying my intentions, especially when that sexy knowing smile curves her lips. In lust. In love. I'm all of it, but I can't ignore that we still have a few hurdles to overcome. Truths to share.

I will tell her before we leave Hamburg, whenever that will be, and even before that, I'll need to disassociate myself from that bank account. But first of all, I need coffee.

―⁓―

I continue to work while Aria reads her book on the small balcony. A mystery. It makes me smile, the fact that she still enjoys the genre when we've only recently had some quieter moments.

They might be the quiet before yet another storm, I think, frowning.

At least I'm making progress, finding more and more proof that Bellini has been trying to trace his wife ever since her disappearance, paid shady PIs and even shadier figures for the job.

Should I be insulted to be added to that list? I suppose I can find comfort in the fact that he didn't choose me personally but asked Rory for recommendations. Still.

Then, Victor came on board, and Bellini changed strategies slightly, but he, too, got the ping on Marina's location in Mexico City. And then Aria took a leap of faith, away from the remnants of her criminal family. On the one hand, he could just let her be, but that's clearly not in his nature. And if she managed to find her mother, he'd have another problem on his hands.

# Chapter Eighteen

## Aria

It's an odd feeling, to halt and think, after spending so many years in a hamster wheel, school, work—I wasn't over- or underappreciated, simply given a job in the corporation that fit my marketing degree, my skill set, and didn't require me to know about any possible illegal activities.

No one at the company ever talked about that, and they didn't blink at the sight of Victor, or the man who had his job before him. I overheard things at family parties, not enough to run to the police and have them all arrested, but rumors. Jokes.

Now I can't help wondering if it was all true. Mom, and later, Dad, used to tell me it was for business reasons that we regularly had lawyers over. Every once in a while, a subpoena couldn't be ignored, but those times were rare, and I was never asked to be there.

Silly? Naive? Perhaps, but given the situation, it might save Mom's life, and mine, once Dad realizes there's nothing I have on him—or Victor.

*He's a killer*, one of my uncles had said with admiration in his tone. That's hardly hard evidence.

I lay the book aside, unable to concentrate on the story.

Saoirse, on the other hand, is extremely focused. I see her at the kitchen table, typing on her phone. She's going over Willow's report again, the one I already read.

My motivation to snoop is surprisingly low. When I saw her in the restaurant, I was attracted to her, but I couldn't know what her agenda was. Risking getting shot at for me definitely changed that, and whatever she might still be keeping from me, I've decided it doesn't matter anymore, because now we have time.

There's still a lot we don't know about each other, and maybe we can find out over time, maybe, at some point, in that cottage in Ireland. I almost laugh at the idea that this would be the fourth country I visit on my trip when I only stopped in Paris before to make sure no one had been on to me. See how that turned out. We are slowing down a bit here in Germany, and the cottage sounds lovely.

Maybe I was a bit predictable, especially if my father already had his eyes on Mom, going after the same clues I had, her friends in Rome.

Ireland? Who would think of us going there?

I try to go back to my book, but I'm distracted by my fantasy, and then, by reminiscing about earlier this morning. Breakfast was delicious too...I'm about to get up, disturb Saoirse's work and remind her that we have some unfinished business too, but I'm holding myself back.

Something tells me she will come to me when the time is right. That, too, is a thrilling thought.

Saoirse rarely asks anyone for anything. That's the impression I get, and yet she's been making inquiries and activating networks to keep me out of Dad's, and therefore, Victor's grasp. Out of the goodness of her heart? I trust that she has a good heart. Does she have other motives? She's determined and a bit possessive, which is oh so attractive to me.

I don't know how much longer I can be patient.

---

I finally pick up the book again, consoling myself with lunch break fantasies—I have a one-track mind these days. The story draws me in, and I keep turning the pages until I look up and realize Saoirse isn't there. I all but jump to my feet, my heart racing, not in a good way now. I step to the window, and nearly faint until I see her by the car, by all appearances looking at something in the trunk.

Okay, calm down. She'll be back in a moment. It shouldn't surprise me so much that I didn't hear her go out. Saoirse sure can be stealthy. It's part of what has kept us from being taken, and worse.

In the kitchen, I pour myself a glass of water, my gaze falling on the report again. Maybe I should read this once more instead of a mystery, but this one is much harder to decipher. Did Mom have help again? How did she manage to slip away? Saoirse's phone is there, partially hidden under the papers. Somehow that strikes me as odd. Didn't I see her with another one, just now, downstairs?

I shouldn't. I really shouldn't. She saved me more than once, and I should leave it at that. What happened to waiting until she's ready to come to me with the rest?

It's not working. I find myself unable to contain my curiosity about my protector's secret. When I see the bank account, the insane sum, and the name attached to it, I can feel my stomach lurch. Keyword: *Retrieval*. Looks like those secrets matter after all.

But...It can't mean what I think it means. My brain can't take all the inconsistencies, make that leap. Something doesn't belong.

Why does Saoirse have access to a bank account that has money transferred to it by a shell company owned by my father? And who the hell is Rory Flynn? No, wait, I've heard that name before, something about his son being murdered. Did Dad do it? Victor? Is Dad paying off Flynn? The thoughts are chasing one another so fast I fail to settle on one.

The pieces still don't come together. If Saoirse took money to bring me back, why the elaborate charade? To make me trust her...and then what? She had expressed such disgust for the violence and the homophobia. If she's still willing to work with them, what does that mean? For her, for me?

My vision blurs abruptly, the emotion stealing my breath. Then I run to the bedroom, where I open my backpack and check the contents. My two passports, money, an extra toothbrush and whatever else a person needs when she has to leave everything else behind, and quickly. I check and realize that Saoirse is still downstairs, making a call. I pack a few more clothes and the book, and then head out of the apartment. There's a backdoor, and I might make it to the street, and to the next subway station from there.

I'm at the end of the hallway when she steps into my path.

"Hey. What's the matter? I was just checking something in the car. We can take a little ride today if you want."

A ride where? To meet with Dad? Victor?

I force a smile. "The car. Right. I saw you outside, and I thought you might want to take a break from those papers. Let's go for a coffee?"

"You don't have to take all this."

"No. I guess." With each passing second, I find it harder to breathe, harder to keep up the semblance of whatever is normal for us. I want to confront her, make her tell me that it's all a big misunderstanding. She has held me when I've cried, made love to me, let me touch her...and yet. "You're right. I think I should invest in a purse. Maybe I was thinking..."

Her gaze softens.

"I have no intel suggesting we can't stay here for a while, so you don't have to take everything you own with you all the time."

"All right. I still should have ID and a bit of money, because I was going to take you out."

Yes, maybe that's a good plan, get out of the house, clear my head, find an explanation for my puzzling find.

Or find an opportunity to get away.

———

Saoirse is quiet but doesn't seem worried at all when we walk to the café two streets away from the building. I'm wearing sneakers. The dress is comfortable enough in case I need to, I don't know, sit on another train for a few hours? I don't want to. I might have to come to terms with the fact that everything I've been dreaming about the past few days was built on a lie.

But why would Dad wait that long...Unless. The realization is like a slap in the face. Unless he was hoping that I'd work with Saoirse to find Mom. Maybe it wasn't for me that she involved all of those connections. All those questions from her and Willow...What if they were trying to get more information out of me, find out what I knew? And for sure, if we found her, Mom might be more open to talk to me than to a stranger.

I'm close to tears again when we enter the café. Just a couple of days ago we sat here holding hands over a latte and a delicious pastry. I hate my life. It's officially the truth, so much more than a throwaway line you might read on the internet. I really do. I thought I had found something genuine, away from the constraints that have come with being Aria Bellini. With her, I could be me.

Maybe I hate her a little, too, but not more than myself. I fell for it again, just like I did when Mom said she loved Dad, and when he told me he'd protect me.

What is it about me that makes it so easy for everyone to lie to me, use me for their own agendas?

When the server comes to our table, Saoirse orders my favorite drink and pastry again.

"What's wrong?" she asks, her tone warm and kind.

"Nothing."

She raises an eyebrow, and I hasten to add. "I swear! I might be coming down with a cold or something. And that book, it might sound silly, but it hit me hard."

"The situation isn't ideal," she acknowledges, and takes my hand. "But I swear, it will change. Soon."

Right. I'm well aware of the irony. A few hours ago, I was dreaming about ravishing her gorgeous body. Against all reason, the touch of her hand has the same effect. I want to be here, with her. The woman I imagined, anyway, not someone who was assigned to me by Dad.

All her vows to protect me...How could I fall for it?

Our order arrives, and the delicious taste and smell make me want to cry too. How could I ever believe there was a way for me out of this nightmare? Forget about settling down somewhere. My life is going to be very much like Mom's, being on the run constantly. At some point, I'll have to find a job, a place to live. With my alternative ID? A haircut? I'm so sick and tired of this. It was never an adventure. Always an illusion.

I pick up the backpack I brought anyway and give her another, hopefully genuine-looking smile. The mere attempt makes my face hurt.

"I'll take this, because I have something else in there...That time of the month."

"Oh. Okay. My sympathies," she says, and I might have laughed, if I hadn't seen that bank information.

I have a very small window of questionable opportunity now, but what if I misunderstood it all?

No, the chance is miniscule, realistically speaking. Not everyone would know to connect the name of that company to Dad's, and the word—*retrieval*? It makes me shudder. Like I'm some sort of package that got lost in the mail.

Everyone lies. Everyone abandons me. I must draw my conclusions from that.

"Yeah. See you in a few."

I chose this café, and our table, because the door of the restroom is out of sight. I gave myself time for a last-minute change of heart.

The bitter sense of betrayal is drowning out everything.

When a group of people from a nearby office building comes in, I slip out unnoticed, and the next moment I'm running.

# Chapter Nineteen

## Saoirse

I knew something more was up with Aria than a heart-wrenching story and, perhaps, a period. In the short time since I met her, I have learned how resilient she really is, so when a few minutes pass by and she doesn't return, I realize I have bigger problems than being stuck with the check for two pastries and specialty coffees. I pay quickly and then head to the restroom, check every stall, not surprised that she isn't there anymore.

Damn it. Did Orlov lie in wait all this time? Did we let down our guards too quickly? I doubt it. If not Rory, Willow would have warned us. That means...

I remember cleaning up the papers from the kitchen table before we left. A glass in the sink. I went outside just for a moment, and Aria didn't move from the couch all morning...

The blood rushes to my face when I remember. That other phone. She couldn't have seen it unless she moved the papers. I've been watching her, and she's been more comfortable, relaxed, has never tried to steal glances...Why now of all times? The one time I left the freaking phone unattended, showing the blood money Bellini was once willing to pay? I wanted to make it go away. To explain to her.

Now I have to find her fast, or I might never get the chance. I hurry back to the house where I find the car untouched. I get into it and start driving. She will likely head to the nearest subway station, and if I don't get there soon, I'll be in trouble. Bellini and Orlov tracked her once, they can do so again, especially if she takes a plane. She won't be able to use cash and prepaid credit cards forever. And I'm afraid of what's going to happen next.

Of course, this is all my fault.

I should have told her sooner, just like I should have put my foot down and insisted that I go with Tommy instead of Hollis. This won't, it can't end like the last time.

I promised her. I promised myself. And I'm going to find her.

I arrive at the station and jog down the stairs to the platform where a train is just arriving. Not a lot of people get on and off here, but I don't see her.

I need a plan B. I call Willow, praying that she's still in Hamburg.

"Please put Kat on speaker," I tell her. "I need a favor, and after that I'll owe you for life."

"Now, let's not go that far...Saoirse? Is everything okay?"

"No," I say. "No, but there's still a chance."

***

I breathe a little easier when so far, despite Bellini's call, there's no indication that Orlov is in Hamburg, or that they even know we are here. That gives me a little time, though I don't have too many illusions as to how much. Willow is well known in the hacker community. Then there are her parents, and Willow's wife. I don't know for sure what they do, and it's certainly above my pay grade, but she knows what it means when I beg her to do everything possible.

To locate Aria. To make sure no one else finds her first.

Rory, predictably, tells me not to meddle.

"I took your advice, and I can tell you, Antonio isn't happy about you breaking the deal."

I want to scream.

"There was never a deal! You dangled that bank account in front of me, remember? I have a lot more information, and it's not good. There's a reason why Bellini's wife did what she did."

At the last moment, I use vague terms. It's probably better not to share with Rory that Marina could be alive when we're not sure Bellini has proof of her living in Mexico. For both of them.

"So, what do you want to do? You can hide her forever."

"Not forever," I say. "Just until they're out of the way."

"Well, good luck, Saoirse. I can't do anything else for you."

"I understand. Thank you."

I mean it, and not just for doing as I said, which, I assume, is no easy feat for the Flynn patriarch. "And give my best to Ciara." We both know that this is goodbye. He's not going to ask me for any more favors. At least he's not asking me for the cottage.

"One more thing. Did you tell Bellini about the cottage?"

"No, why would I? That has nothing to do with anything."

It's not his place to be this indignant, but at least he's genuine. I appreciate that more than he will ever know.

"Again, thank you."

There's a small pause. I end the call. There's no time to rehash the past or what could have been. This part of my story is over, though I suppose the property will always serve as a reminder.

I could be happy there, but first I must convince Aria that I'd give my life to save her, and that we still have a future.

While I'm waiting for information, I drive around in case she chose a less predictable option earlier. It doesn't make sense though—the subway is how she would get across the city the quickest. I hope she's not hitchhiking.

Damn it, Aria, why didn't you wait for me? I was almost done getting rid of that account. Bellini's money would have been nice had he really been just a father concerned for his daughter's well-being. That theory went out of the window the moment he paid men who tried to drag her into a car, and Victor to take her off his hands.

And then there's the more difficult part I haven't even told her. If Willow is right, Aria isn't his. She likely isn't going to inherit a dime from that fortune, but Marina still could—this is why he wants Aria, because he thinks he can get to Marina through her. If her mother is gone, he doesn't have to worry about any of it. I'm sure that Victor is just as much a means to an end, to eventually produce an heir to the Bellini name.

I remember Rory and Ciara fawning over Courtney's son, fantasizing about his future in the family business. Everything is a whole lot worse in Aria's family. At least Courtney wanted a child and a family. Bellini doesn't give a shit about what Aria wants.

As I wait for information from Willow, I call Ryan Farmer, who, naturally, isn't amused.

"Ms. Reilly," she says. "Where the hell are you? I assume you didn't take time zones into consideration either." Despite the challenging situation, I have to smile.

"I'm sorry about that. I figured you didn't need me for anything anymore. I, on the other hand, needed a break. Anyway, that's not important. You know someone who has eyes on Antonio Bellini?"

She gets very quiet all of a sudden. "Why are you asking me that?"

"If that isn't the case, you should. You should also look into the disappearance of his wife who was last seen in Mexico five months ago. I'd be willing to leave the woman alone, but her daughter is missing as well, and we can't have Daddy find her first. Can you get on that?"

"Yes, Ma'am, immediately."

"That's great, thank you so—"

"No! No, I can't get on it, just because you say so," she returns, not hiding her irritation. Well, good luck with that. I'm irritated too.

"Listen to me, her life is in danger. If Bellini is occupied at home, and he calls his guard dog back, we'll be okay. I won't bother you anymore, I swear."

"We, huh? I'm not sure what you imagine my work to be, but I can't go off on my own like that. Bellini isn't our jurisdiction. I can put out the word to another field office, but I can't promise—"

"He's trying to get to Aria though her mother and bury the truth with her. They are both in danger."

"Saoirse, if you could just come in and tell me everything you know..." She tries a different angle now. I recognize the tactic.

"There's no time," I say and end the call, just before my phone buzzes with a text.

Aria has checked into a hotel, using her credit card. Maybe she's just as tired as I am.

I have to hurry. Everything will be okay. This time, my smile is genuine.

I send a prayer of gratitude to whatever deity gave Willow her mad skills.

It's not too late.

# Chapter Twenty

## Aria

I'm not sure how, but I made it. At the subway station, I changed my mind last minute and took a cab. Not the best choice money wise, but I got away anyway. I ask the driver to drop me off in the city center, and that, too, might not the wisest choice.

I don't know anyone here, I still have a precarious sense of orientation, but I couldn't bring myself to leave Hamburg yet. Silly, I know. But what if Victor doesn't show up here, and there's another explanation for that bank account?

I find a medium-priced hotel and check in, automatically pay with my credit card. Add that to my not so wise choices, but I need to do something on my side to end this, see what happens, draw them out?

I can't wait, can't hide for the rest of my life. What's more, I don't want to. When I sit down on the bed in the room that, while not that spacious, feels too big and silent already, I know that whatever Saoirse's agenda was, she has already given me more than she might have ever intended.

A taste of freedom that goes beyond cutting ties with my father, far beyond trying to solve the mystery that is my mother.

I had a glimpse of what the future could be like with someone by my side, someone who cares...This, apparently, wasn't it. Still, I'm as amazed at what it was, as I'm grieving all the things that were never real except in my fantasy. I don't know what to think or believe, but I know I need to wait this out, formulate a plan of my own.

If I went to a police station and told my story...I abandon that thought immediately. I wouldn't believe it myself if confronted with those wild facts. They might contact Dad. They might think I was crazy for trusting Saoirse in the first place. Maybe I was, lusting after her, thinking her motives might be completely altruistic. She mentioned her friend a couple of times. She gave me little hints that not everything was as it seemed.

And I... I couldn't get out of my clothes fast enough around her. I miss her already, the closeness, the conversations and the silence, the laughter we shared despite the looming complications.

What an act, to take me to various safehouses across Europe. She mentioned going back home before, but never pushed that hard. What it all meant...I might never know.

I do remember that name though, Rory Flynn, and do some Internet research. His business is the import of whiskey, and it's seen some rough times since a supposedly botched delivery got guests at a hotel in his city sick. Then, the story of his son. I didn't know, but apparently, he was killed by a corrupt cop.

More recently, the authorities investigated Flynn regarding any possible involvement in his daughter-in-law's kidnapping, but it seems like those charges didn't stick. There's an older picture of him and his wife Ciara, his son Tommy, the afore-mentioned daughter-in-law holding a baby in her arms. This doesn't help me except...In the background I see a familiar face, back straight, her expression unreadable, Saoirse Reilly looks like she's guarding the family.

More mysteries.

Why is Flynn's name on that bank account? Is he the friend Saoirse mentioned, and why would he know about me and my troubles unless...I didn't get the impression that Dad was very fond of Irish mobsters, but I also know he will associate with anyone if he thinks it can further his agenda, Victor a case in point. I'm both fascinated and appalled.

Did Saoirse play the same role for the Flynns that Victor does for our family? Does she still? Is she involved in similar crimes?

My instincts tell me otherwise. When I was with her, I felt safe, never had that lingering sensation of terror that I had around Victor, something I couldn't even admit to myself until I put some distance between us. That cottage in Ireland she mentioned, was it part of her compensation? Damn it, I wish I could ask her all those questions. I want to.

I'm not sure if I'm brave enough.

Meanwhile, I'll wait. For what, I'm not quite sure.

Where could I go from here? No need to go back to Rome when it's fairly certain Mom isn't there anymore.

I open the browser again and look at trains and planes leaving tonight.

Is there anywhere Dad or Victor don't have connections?

I laugh bitterly.

Australia maybe, but I'm not at that point yet.

No. Right now, I might not be in danger of getting married off, but this isn't a life either. And I won't let them determine mine.

I still have an ace or two up my sleeve.

# Chapter Twenty-One

## Saoirse

I have to be careful, not spook her. At the same time, I have to be quick, make sure we can leave as soon as possible. I wish I could convince her to go home for a bit, as I believe the odds would be on our side. Willow and Kat will also be back in the States by then, and I have more law enforcement contacts. It's either that, or we return to the place that felt home the moment I walked through the door. I'm still hopeful enough to imagine she could feel the same.

I park the car a couple of streets away—we'll have to abandon it anyway. Then I approach the hotel on foot, head past the lobby to the elevator and up to the third floor where her room is located.

I knock. It's not like she'll jump out of the window, and she'll have to get out at some point. No room service here.

"Aria, it's me," I say when there's no sound coming from the inside. "Please. We need to talk. I know I need to explain a few things to you."

"No kidding."

Has she been waiting by the door? Maybe it's really small inside.

"So, that's why you didn't want my money. Dad already took care of it. Is Victor with you? Were you in on it together?"

"God, no," I return, my stomach lurching at the idea. "I've never talked to Victor or your father. Rory told me the story about how your father's business partners had made threats against you, and I was supposed to find you before they made good on those threats. I realized soon enough it was all bullshit."

On the other side of the door, Aria is silent.

"I didn't take the money. I told Rory I didn't want it. He's starting to understand what's going on, and he's not going to rat us out."

"Like he did in the beginning. That's how they kept finding us."

Not the best moment to indulge, but she's undoubtedly smart. I am proud of her. I don't want any more obstacles between us, words, truths, this damn door.

"I guess so. But I convinced him that your father is not the best person to do business with."

"Good for you. The Flynns still matter to you, don't they?"

"I worked for them a long time. I quit a few months ago, but when Rory called me, I really thought you were in immediate danger...and I won't lie, at the time, the money didn't hurt either. Let me in, please?"

More hesitation, then she finally opens the door.

"Thank you. I swear to you, I can explain, but first we need to get out of here. It's not safe."

"You know, for the last few days, I trusted you to tell me what was safe and what was not. I'm not so sure anymore, Saoirse."

I deserved that.

"Why are you here? Why did you jump at the chance to find a random woman when you didn't even know the whole story?"

"I thought I did." She has a point, but we don't have time to discuss it now. "I made a mistake, but there's still time to correct it. When I thought I could help...I couldn't say no."

"Does Flynn have something over you?"

"No, no, he doesn't, other than he and his wife took me in and gave me opportunities when my own parents...Let's say it was a volatile situation at home. I owed them, but I did more than pay them back over the years. They gave me your picture and told me that those business partners might try to kill you. I couldn't let that happen."

She takes a step closer.

"Why?" she whispers.

I want nothing more than to come clean completely, have glorious make up sex with her in this hotel room, but the footsteps in the hallway remind me that we have other issues to address first, and fast.

"Grab your backpack. Let's make a run for it one more time, and I swear I'll tell you everything."

"What if we don't run anymore? What if we confront them?"

"I don't think that's a good idea right now. We need more of a plan if we want to do that. I have people who are helping back home, but Aria, I need you to come with me now."

She grabs her backpack which is leaning against the wall by the door, and we head away from the sound of the footsteps and to the stairs. We should be able to make it, I think, my mind still reeling from the rapid development of the past few hours. Maybe it's better that way. There is no going back. If we want to be free, we have to pool all our resources, uncover the whole truth, put Bellini and Orlov in their place—a prison cell, hopefully.

I dare a small smile in Aria's direction as we run down the stairs, almost thinking she's going to roll her eyes at me. We're on the ground floor and head toward the door leading to the lobby. Aria is a few steps ahead of me, her hand already on the handle when she turns to me, and I see her eyes widen.

The sharp pain at the back of my head is sudden, cruel, and the last sensation before consciousness vanishes. The last sentiment, regret, is even worse.

# Chapter Twenty-Two

## Aria

I don't stop screaming until Victor slaps me across the face, and the other man holds a gun to Saoirse's head after removing hers from the inside of her coat, along with her phones, and wallet. Is she even still alive? All of a sudden, I'm frozen in shock, unable to move.

"What the hell did you do? What did you do that for?" I haven't lost my speech though.

He ignores me.

Everything has happened so fast. We had almost made it, and then that goon hit her, and Victor pulled me away from the door. They came from another hallway where more rooms are located. Someone, guests, staff, have to come through here? Maybe someone heard a commotion and will call the police?

"Go check with the others and make sure they searched the room," Victor tells the other man. "I'll take care of her."

They were waiting for us down here in the stairwell, cutting off our escape before we could make it to the lobby and outside. I have to think, and fast.

When it's just the two of us, he gives me a smile that turns my stomach.

"It's so good to see you again, Aria. I was starting to think you were avoiding me."

"Keep your hands off me," I warn him.

"Or what? You'll tell Daddy? We both know that he'd very much like me to get my hands on you. We could be married in a matter of days. Now, let's get out of here."

"No. She needs a doctor."

Of course, he has a gun too. So predictable. Dad paid for an army of security guards, but I never had a single self-defense class. That's an oversight, sadly, on my part.

"Sweetheart, the time of saying no is over. Or do you want me to end this right here?"

He trains the gun on her, and I can't breathe. I nearly throw up, but I shake my head.

"Will you be quiet, give her a chance? The next time an employee comes through here, they might be able to save her."

"Yes." The docile tone is a soft, thin surface, hiding my rage behind. He will pay for this. If I had the opportunity, I wouldn't hesitate one second. I hated him before, but now there are no bounds. Except, I have to get out of this first.

"Good. We always knew you would come around. It won't be so bad, I promise. You'll have all the books, dresses, and shoes your little heart desires, and nothing else to worry about."

Does he actually hear himself? The sarcasm doesn't even come close to piercing the choking fear, and I put one step in front of the other, robotic, knowing I can't defy him as long as Saoirse isn't safe. One call to the other minion, and they will likely kill her. They might anyway, but I can't allow myself to think that, to give up. She came for me, more than once. I have to do what I can for her now.

There's no one behind the reception desk, just a young woman with a toddler sitting in the lobby. Our eyes meet briefly, but I don't try anything, to scared I might drag some innocent bystander into the mess I created. Victor's smug smile tells me he can guess what's on my mind.

"Good girl," he mutters, and a few violent fantasies are coursing through my mind.

Outside the hotel, there's an SUV with tinted windows waiting. He opens the door for me. I want to run. I can't.

When I sit inside, my jaw drops at the man beside me.

"Aria. It's about time you came home," Dad says as the driver pulls out of the parking lot. I have no idea where he's driving us.

Saoirse talked about people in the US being able to help. Someone like Willow? But she's not police. Rory Flynn? Is there anyone I will be able to turn to, if I get the chance at all?

Anyone to help me wake up from this nightmare.

"Where are we going? And what do you mean? I'm on vacation. As we've discussed."

His face darkens, and it takes me a whole lot of restraint not to shrink away. Sure, I've heard him yell sometimes on the phone, with business partners behind closed doors. Until a few months ago, or even recently, I was able to maintain a certain image of him in my mind. It's dead, gone. This is the man who has been chasing first Mom, then me, all over Europe.

I can't help wondering what it is that Saoirse wanted to tell me, what she found out. I might never know. And if it's all my fault, for running away in the first place.

But that money...How could I have known?

I suppose there's a way for me to find out now.

"You wasted that money for nothing, by the way."

"Because Reilly is a dyke?"

I would laugh if I wasn't so scared. It's all so predictable, and yes, laughable. There's prejudice in families like mine, no doubt about it.

"What does that have to do with anything? You put money in that bank account. She found me. Why hurt her?"

I can't help it, maybe a part of me hopes to wear him down if I just keep shooting questions at him.

"I don't owe you any answers," he replies. "You, on the other hand, have a lot to answer for."

"Are you serious? You sicced an Irish mob boss on me, along with your favorite Russian doll."

I don't care if it's inappropriate, I'm tired and scared and itching for a fight, all at once. And I sure as hell don't give a damn about hurting the feelings of any of these men.

"What the hell were you thinking anyway, sneaking away from Victor?" he asks, anger receding now that he has me where he wants me. "You really thought you were smart enough?"

"Well, if I'm lacking any smarts, I guess I know who's to blame."

Stop it. Aria, for the love of God, stop.

To my surprise, he starts laughing. In fact, he's bursting with laughter.

"No, sorry about that, but whatever you're lacking, you should put that squarely on your mother, the whore."

His bigotry might be predictable, but this crosses a line. He anticipates my move and catches my wrist before I can hit him. I can hear Victor snicker in the front passenger seat, while the driver remains stoic and unimpressed.

"I guess I should have known when Reilly didn't touch the money. Silly girl, that one. Did she tell you that your grand-parents bribed me into marrying your mother when she was pregnant and had nowhere to go?"

That silences me. Perhaps she would have, had there been enough time. He might be lying. Then again...a lot of things make sense now, and yet, the set-up becomes even more confusing.

"And now you want to get back at my dead grandparents by marrying me off to that head minion of yours? I'm sorry, Dad, that doesn't make any sense. I know you don't care about me, or Mom, but you could have just let us go! Mom obviously doesn't care about money. I don't want it either. So, what the hell do you want from me?"

"Watch your mouth, first of all." Oh, the audacity of a man who called my mother a whore. "That will be for Victor to address shortly. We will make arrangements as soon as we are home."

"No! This is not going to happen!"

My father's smile chills me to the bone. He reaches into the pocket of his suit jacket, and I retreat to the farthest corner of the car when he produces a syringe.

"You seem to have taken a liking to Reilly. Don't forget that we still have eyes on her."

I have a vision of opening that door and jumping into traffic.

Just like I expected, it's locked. There's no way out for me.

# Chapter Twenty-Three

## Saoirse

I'm so angry I can barely breathe, the sentiment all-encompassing before I even open my eyes. I force myself into a sitting position, catching the red stain on the carpet on the periphery of my vision. My head hurts so bad it's hard to think, let alone focus on the hotel employee speaking to me in rapid German, communicating her shock clearly in her tone and expression.

*"Um Gottes Willen, was ist mit Ihnen passiert? Bitte, halten Sie still. Der Krankenwagen wird gleich hier sein."*

I ignore her and struggle to my feet. What happened to me? It's a good question, but I don't have time for any of it. I can't stay still and wait for the ambulance, or reassure the woman.

"I need to make a call!" Several calls, actually. "My phone was stolen. Could you please…?"

"Oh, of course. Excuse me, please. There you go." She hands me her phone, obviously assuming I'd call a loved one. I send a few texts with the same message.

*This is SR. Invoking emergency protocol.* That sounds a whole lot more official than it actually is, but it will inform my allies that things have gotten out of hand and could get worse by the minute. I know I need to get to the airport. I'm certain that Victor plans to take Aria back to the States, and he will use any means possible to achieve that goal. If I'm lucky, I can catch up with them first. If not...A lot can happen in the time it takes to fly over the Atlantic. I'd rather not take that chance.

"Thank you. That's all I need."

I'm standing, that's all that matters. I can hear the sirens and know I have to make my escape. I don't want to deal with the police either. There is no time to explain the whole, complicated story.

"*Aber...Sie koennen doch so nicht einfach gehen!*"

I can leave, and I will.

"I'm sorry. Thank you again!" I am in the lobby and out on the street where the ambulance has just pulled up in front of the hotel. I see a couple of guests giving me a strange look, then I open the door of a cab and tell him, "*Zum Flughafen, bitte.*"

―⁓―

I must have gotten hit harder than I thought, because I realize too late that I won't get further than the security line without a credit card or a passport. Has the safehouse been compromised, or did they only find Aria because of her credit card? In any case, they were already here, and they were fast.

After some back and forth with the cab driver who threatens to call the police when he realizes I can't pay, I squeeze out some tears which isn't hard to do and tell him in broken German about running from an abusive boyfriend. At least, there are enough elements of the truth in there to convince him to lend me his phone, and I am lucky. I can have someone retrieve some cash and my passport from the safehouse and bring it. After that...I check my emails while the driver regards me with a mix of suspicion and pity.

It's Kat who arrives only a half hour later, grumpy as usual, but she has everything I asked for. I could swear she flinched a little when she saw me, but I can pay the driver and then some, and send him on his way.

"What's the plan?"

I nearly admit then and there that I don't have much of one, and I feel like lying down and not getting up in the immediate future.

"I have to figure out where they went," I say. "I'm certain they'll try to take her back."

"You might be right."

"Do you know anything?" I tried to clean myself up in the cab, but when I reach up behind my head, my fingers still come away wet.

"Nothing concrete," she says. "But we think Bellini might try to avoid taking her through security here."

"They don't have a choice, do they?"

"Normally they wouldn't. We are looking at private jets at the moment. There's been talk that Bellini has ties to a German politician who could arrange things for him."

A politician in another country, of course.

Fuck him and his money, and his endless resources. Not that I'm surprised. When the dominos start to fall, it will impact a whole lot more people than Bellini and Orlov. The authorities will seize a vast portion of that fortune, not that I think Aria cares.

"So, what are we waiting for?"

"Saoirse. You're not in particularly good shape." She holds up a hand when I start to protest. "There are still some things we have to confirm, but there's not much more we can do from here. We'll be better off trying to get her out on the other side of the Atlantic."

My vision blurs for a brief moment. I've felt like this before, and I can't ever go this deep again, into the pain and regret. I won't make it out. But this isn't about me. I won't make a mistake this time.

"A lot can happen in the time it takes to get there."

She doesn't disagree. "You and Flynn came to an understanding?"

"We did."

"What about that FBI lady?"

"I've informed everyone, as much as I could between getting hit over the head and coming here."

"Good. They'll know to watch out on their side. Saoirse, there's more."

There always is. I'm so tired, but I can't rest until Aria is safe with me.

"I think we have a lead on her mother," Kat says.

"That's great," I say. "We'll deal with it later."

---

I hate waiting. For our flight to board, the plane to take off, the hours spent in the air. Willow has joined us as they are on their way home as well, and she'll come with me to a meeting I've scheduled for as soon as we get out of the airport on the other side.

This is the one shot we have.

We've confirmed that Bellini is taking Aria home on a private plane, and if he succeeds, he'll continue to hold her hostage, only things will be much worse. Maybe it's the head injury, but I still feel like we are missing pieces of the puzzle.

Is it Aria's biological father? Why would Bellini think he has to find her mother and have Aria marry Victor to protect his fortune, when neither woman has any interest in him or said fortune? Is he just too far gone to imagine that there are people out there who just want to live their lives?

These questions aren't priority, getting Aria out of the clutches of these cruel men is—but I can't help thinking that the answers might help us achieve that goal.

Kat gives me a stern look when I have the flight attendant give me a whiskey with my Ginger Ale for the second time. I glare back at her. If this wasn't so important, I'd take it neat, and it wouldn't be the second only.

Willow touches her arm lightly, and she backs down from the silent standoff.

I still want to cry. It's not yet time to indulge myself.

# Chapter Twenty-Four

## Aria

"Wake up, sleeping beauty. Lunch time."

I shrink away from the touch to my cheek, and the too cheerful voice. Victor is in a good mood now that he has completed the job my father gave him.

I can no longer pretend I'm still out, so I blink cautiously, then wish I hadn't. We're on a private plane. I know that he charters one on occasion, and apparently, he didn't want to try putting a drugged woman on a commercial flight. Still, this is beyond. Didn't we have to go through security?

Then again, Antonio Bellini always makes sure that people owe him, so he can make them bend the rules for him when it's convenient.

"Cat got your tongue? Well, you have plenty of time to wake up, but then we'll have things to talk about."

I don't know if it's the remnants of the drug, the smell of food, or the sudden turbulence—maybe all three—but my stomach can't cope with my situation any longer. There's a grim satisfaction in puking all over his shoes, though it doesn't last.

His face reddens as he stumbles backwards, almost losing his footing because of the ongoing turbulence. A seasoned flight attendant gets me a warm, wet washcloth before she, too, has to take a seat and fasten her seatbelt.

"Ever the dramatic one, Aria," Dad says. "Taking after your mother." He doesn't seem to be perturbed by the turbulence. I'm more angry than anything, because these are the last people I want to be with now. The last people to...I can't think like that. Saoirse has many resources too, and she will figure out what happened. She won't leave me here, unless...

As the plane lurches, worst case scenarios course through my mind. If she's alive—no, scratch that, there's no if. She has to be. But she might be hurt badly, or even have amnesia. She might have forgotten about me.

I stubbornly blink back the tears. I made it all the way to Paris, evaded them for a while with Saoirse's help, I can do it again. But this time, I have to be even better at fooling them, because they won't let me out of their sight. I can do it, and I will.

There's no way I'm going to become Mrs. Orlov. Over my dead body, it's not an exaggeration.

I've made mistakes too, and I need to redeem myself the first chance I can get. I lean back in my seat, and until the skies clear, I dream about our life in that small quaint cottage.

---

Once the seatbelt sign is off, I go see the flight attendant, and I'm not surprised when she provides me with a toothbrush, toothpaste and a change of clothes. I feel a bit less wobbly, body and mind, after I'm all cleaned up. She's even heating up some lunch for me I refused earlier—not to be contrary, but I wasn't sure my stomach could handle it. Victor is working now, which is a relief. I know that Dad is watching me, and I try to pretend I'm not so hyper-aware of it.

To my surprise, I am actually hungry, and the tea helps too. I need to keep up the pretense for as long as I can, for the moment a chance presents itself. I don't know yet when that will be. I have to be ready.

I'm stalling, drinking more tea. I can't be too obvious—Dad will see right through it. He doesn't trust me right now, and I have to think quick. He doesn't care about me either, never did, so I guess the best I can do is to appeal to his ego.

"I guess I wasn't that good at this after all," I say. "Could you tell me at least how you found me?"

"Found you?" He laughs. Somehow, a lot of this seems to strike him as funny.

I swallow my anger.

"That idiot Flynn made it easy. He's so desperate he bent over backwards to be of service."

"And he sent Ms. Reilly." My heart is beating faster, nausea threatening again when I think of the last time I saw her.

"She had her own agenda, obviously. But don't worry, Victor won't mind."

Next, I'm going to puke on *his* shoes.

"Lucky me, then. You sent him to kill her?"

I am not that bad. The words come out rather light, conversational. I want to punch him, and Victor, but I know my limits. With still about three hours to go, this would only end badly.

"Kill her? No, Reilly is alive and well. Maybe not well, as I assume she'll be terribly jealous, but that's not our problem, is it? I think once word is out that your wedding is imminent, not even your mother will want to miss it."

I mull this over, wrapping all that fear and nausea into a layer of ice. I pray that he's not lying about Saoirse.

"Really? I know you don't owe me any answers, not that you've ever given me one, but I can't help being curious. She left such a long time ago, never even tried to contact me. What makes you think she cares about my wedding?"

"Oh, I know she cares," he says with a smile. "And for your information, she did try to contact you, that foolish woman. More than once. That's how we almost found her."

I almost lose my already shaky composure over this. In all those years, Dad rarely took the time to talk to me about subjects other than meals, parties, school and then, my job at the company. It usually came down to small talk, the rest was left to his employees.

The realization of how utterly alone I was from the moment she left, until Saoirse stepped into my life, is staggering. In the years between, there were few friends, no one close, no one I could really talk to. A few brief encounters, and the artist who painted me. I think she's married now.

I never knew that Mom had still been thinking about me.

Almost. That means they are still looking.

"I guess me going to Rome was helpful too."

He shrugs. "You didn't have enough information. We've had eyes on Emilia and her parents for a while, but we weren't sure whether Marina was planning to come back there. This, she won't be able to resist."

"You want to kill her?"

Victor is still focused on the screen of the laptop. I hate his little condescending smile.

"What did I tell you about being melodramatic?" Dad is amused, but his tone has softened since we got here.

I am succeeding.

"Sorry about that. You scared me in Rome."

"I'm not planning on killing either of you," he says. "All I want is for her to come back so we can throw you a lovely wedding, and we can all be a happy family again."

At this point, it's hard to know who's delusional, but there's one thing I know for certain. I want to spend the rest of my life as far away from him as possible.

That, and he needs to pay for all the pain he's caused.

---

It's like I never left. I'm back in my suite. It looks, smells the same, has probably been cleaned in my absence, the scent of air freshener family.

My prison guard outside the door. At least it still locks, which is giving me the illusion of safety. I have no phone, no access to the Internet. It doesn't sit well with me that all I can do is wait. I have done so for years, and I don't want to waste another minute of my life.

All I can do at the moment is get ready for dinner as my father has asked me to. He has guests, and has already told me not to bother trying to stage something:

Don and Lillian Aiello won't care. Their names are familiar from previous parties. They, too, have a daughter, but I've rarely seen her since she's spent most of her time away in boarding schools and then, university in Europe. Frankly, I don't give a damn, and likely, neither does she.

I do change into appropriate attire though, knowing that Victor will be close by, leering, from the moment I open the door, to when I'll come back later tonight.

So far, nothing much has happened, but I'm not that naïve. It's bad that I couldn't get away at the airport. It will be so much harder from here, but I have to trust in myself, assure myself that I can fool them.

If I allow only a moment of contemplating the alternative, the fear will be paralyzing.

Reluctantly, I turn the key, and sure enough, Victor is waiting, wearing the kind of suit that tells me he'll be at the table tonight.

"Ready, my dear fiancée?"

He takes my arm, and I force a smile, proud of my acting skills when I don't recoil. I console myself with fantasies of hurting him in a sensitive place.

Nothing has changed in this house, and yet, it feels like I've been gone forever. I can't afford to waver now. I must focus, but when we sit in the stuffy dining room, joined by Dad's friends, Mr. and Mrs. Aiello and their daughter, I can't help daydreaming of those places Saoirse and I went together: the restaurants and coffee shops, evening walks in foreign cities where everything and everyone felt more like home than this.

Does this set-up really impress anyone? Dad certainly hopes so, because the way he's kissing up to Aiello is embarrassing. I remember his words about Flynn, Saoirse's former employer. He's one to talk.

Ruby Aiello keeps her gaze mostly on her plate. She doesn't want to be here any more than I do, and I can't help wondering what her parents told her. She's close to my age. Did they pick a husband for her too?

All of a sudden, an idea forms in my mind. I'm aware of Victor watching me closely, wearing that little patronizing smile that does little to cover up the fact that he slapped me yesterday, will do worse if this goes on longer. I could just...I don't know, she's bound to have a phone? Try to contact Saoirse somehow, or Willow, or Rory Flynn? I'm not quite sure how, without having any of their phone numbers, but she might be willing to help?

Or she isn't. I can't figure her out, and I don't have enough time.

Victor stops his hovering for a moment and gets up to leave the room, a glance passing between him and Dad. I nearly sigh in relief when his hovering presence is gone. Ruby looks up from her plate and our eyes meet, but I still can't read her.

We finish the main course and sit in silence interspersed by the men's boasting about this or that achievement over their competitors.

Eventually, Ruby excuses herself for the restroom. I take a deep breath, force myself to wait a few seconds.

As if reading my thoughts, Victor is back, his hand heavy on my shoulder, his grip firm enough to make me wince. He hands me another glass of wine.

"I don't think I—"

"You don't want to cause trouble," he mutters. "Because that would be foolish."

Oh, I want to, but I can't trust our guests enough to get me out of this. Ruby, maybe. Lillian, she's cold enough to make me shudder. I take a careful sip, then another, having a hard time not to feel like all hope is slipping away.

It doesn't take long for the sounds around me to fade out. They're distant now, as if I'm under water. It's a strange sensation, like floating.

It's not just my feeling. My situation is hopeless. I hear Dad telling the Aiellos about me not having adjusted to my medication yet, mixing it with alcohol, and that my upcoming wedding will certainly cure my depression.

They toast to it, while Ruby looks uncomfortable. She won't meet my eyes anymore.

# Chapter Twenty-Five

## Saoirse

The people here have never been in the same room together before, and they present the most unusual alliance. It would be fascinating if I wasn't hurting so badly, questioning the wisdom of my afternoon drinking. Not that it made me tipsy, but it didn't help with anything else either.

They're uneasy, I know, but I couldn't care less about their feelings.

Only Willow seems fairly relaxed. Agent Farmer's scowl reminds me of Kat who isn't present now, and Rory tries to keep up the pretense of holding all the cards, when we all know he messed up. Again.

The problem is that when lesser evils are toppled, worse try to move in. I don't know that I ever considered him evil, but he certainly has his flaws.

"I can't tell any of you about an ongoing investigation," Farmer states.

"No one's asking you to."

"I can't condone or stay silent about anything illegal you might plan either."

"Yeah, right, we follow you," Rory says, and she glares at him.

"The question is, how do we get to Aria?" Willow says softly, and I send a grateful smile her way.

"Yes, thank you, that's the entire point here. All I need is for him to be distracted, best case scenario, away for a few hours. I can deal with Orlov."

"Not by yourself, you can't," Rory argues. "You need back-up."

"This is all crazy. You can't do anything," Farmer returns. "If she's held there, we will investigate."

"There's no if. They tried to take her in Rome, then came after us a couple of times, until Hamburg. He did this to me," I hold up my hand to touch the bandage. "This is the man her father wants Aria to marry as soon as legally possible. I don't think he gives a damn about whether it helps him with anything. He just wants to hurt her, and make no mistake, Orlov will."

In my lap, my fingers flex. I can't stand to sit around here any longer.

"It is now or never. We know she's there, and that it will get more dangerous the longer she stays with those awful people. Look, I understand I owe all of you a great deal. I'm aware. But frankly I don't give a damn about any legalities or alliances. You help me or not, your choice."

All of a sudden, the air seems calmer. There's an understanding. I don't know Ryan Farmer's whole story, or Willow's, for that matter, but I'm sure Rory is thinking of Tommy, wishing he could have a second chance. Maybe he even regrets his lack of action regarding Courtney, but I'm probably being too optimistic. I don't care. I have them on my side.

"And this is how we'll do it."

In the end, Ryan Farmer will be protected from the fallout. We all know that without her ever so slightly in our corner, the future is pretty much doomed. Willow has her mad hacking skills, an unbelievable amount of money, and Kat to protect her, and Rory...Well, I guess he still has contacts. It helps that he's grudgingly been coming to the conclusion that the feuds of old truly don't work anymore, and that good deeds will help keep him out of prison, and perhaps, see his grandson every once in a while.

He told me that Courtney is still angry. I don't blame her, but it's not my story to rectify.

Before we leave, the agent takes me aside.

"Are you sure you're up for this?" she asks me. "You're in over your head."

"Something tells me that's a state you can relate to. You're married, right?"

She tenses, even though it's certainly not a secret.

"Then you know what it's like. Because you couldn't live with yourself if you hadn't tried everything to save the person you love."

"Love?" she returns, and I realize I caught her by surprise. Myself, too, at least by saying it out loud, to someone who's not more than an acquaintance to me. "You've known her for how long?"

"Irrelevant," I scoff. "And I'm fine. I've survived worse." Maybe one day we'll all sit down together, just the women, perhaps including Courtney even, and reflect on that over a sufficient amount of booze. Once this is over.

Make no mistake, it will be soon.

I have no illusions when, about twenty minutes later, I sit in the car by myself. It's a good thing I can pretty much drive anything, since for the last few months I had to make do with whatever was available from rental companies and allies.

Farmer pointed out that perhaps I shouldn't even be driving tonight, let alone lead a rescue mission. She might have a point though she didn't try to argue hard when I reminded her of her own stakes.

I might be lucky, but I'm aware that when it comes down to it, I'll be alone, success or failure. Agent Farmer has her security net to fall back on. Willow's wealth more than matches Bellini's. I never asked, and I'm not sure I'd get an answer.

Rory—well, things can never be the same. I just prefer not to have him as my enemy in this.

They will all do their part, but in the end it's up to me. And there's only one acceptable outcome, because I couldn't live with myself otherwise. No matter what Aria chooses. Of course, it will be her decision whether she'll cut all ties with the family name or try to clean up if she gets the chance. Lives out loud or leads a quiet life here, or anywhere else she has ties, family or friends. Maybe she'll want to let Emilia know once it's safe for her and her parents.

Or we could make it come true, burn all bridges and move to the cottage...I'm not even sure Aria would want that after I failed to keep her with me, keep her safe, but I want a chance to ask her at least. At the same time, we'll have to have a conversation about what Willow unearthed about Bellini. Maybe she could even find Aria's biological father, but that's a subject for another day.

The plan came together in record time. Willow has set up at the location where we met earlier. She'll be my eyes and ears. Rory's job is to lure Bellini away, and Ryan Farmer, well, she can't say too much, but as soon as any crimes are confessed or committed, she'll be ready to swoop in. It's all very limited in scope, so every minute counts.

I park the car in the spot we agreed on, from where I'll be able to see Rory and Bellini leave. The cameras at the gate and motion detectors will be disabled, thanks to Willow.

My mind is calm and clear now, the headache almost gone. I know what I have to do, without doubts or theatrics. This is my chance.

The headlights appear right on cue, and I know Rory and Bellini are on their way. I sink a bit deeper in my seat as they drive past me. I can't tell what the atmosphere in the car is like, but from the distance, it doesn't look too tense. Good. We are taking a huge chance. Then again, I know that Rory, while he has pissed off men like Bellini before, is also the type who can put them at ease when he wants to. He'll be fine.

I exit the car and move in, Willow's voice in my ear. It's easy to get to the gate and through it. On the other side, I have to pay a whole lot more attention.

"Three o' clock, armed guard," she warns me.

"I see him."

I am armed too, but I don't want to risk engaging this early. This guy will still be making the rounds when I'm inside, and if all works well, we'll be gone by the time he realizes what's going on. But of course, he's not the only one.

And there's Victor Orlov. Recalling the last encounter, I wince, even more determined. Payback would be lovely, though I can hold off on that until Aria is safe and sound. After that, all bets are off with the bastard.

# Chapter Twenty-Six

## Aria

I hate them so much. I think at this point I even hate Ruby Aiello and her family for accepting that this kind of thing could be normal, that families behave this way. I am so tired, not quite nauseated enough to ruin anyone's shoes again, but there's a constant queasiness.

Victor has steered me to the couch, and when our guests are about to leave, I don't even manage more than a lopsided smile.

Ruby shakes my hand which makes me pause.

"Nice to see you again, Aria. Maybe we could have a coffee sometime soon."

"Yes, maybe," I whisper.

"Come on," Lillian cuts in. "You'll see her at the wedding. If only you could contribute a bit more to the conversation every once in a while, she might even make you the maid of honor."

Ruby winces, while Dad laughs and pats her shoulder. "That's a wonderful idea. We shall talk about this some more soon. Lillian, I'm so grateful for your help. It's not easy without a woman in the house, and poor Aria...I'm sorry about all this. She'll do better."

Against all odds, I feel embarrassed, and that makes me even angrier. I'm sure the Aiellos think there's a good reason why Dad plans to never let me outside again.

Of course, the wedding will be held on our own grounds. Well, his. It looks like I, or Mom, never really owned anything. Much of his crusade was about obsession, possessiveness. And he's about to win. That's not giving up, it's realistic, right?

I just hope Saoirse is okay, that she'll be able to have a life away from all this crap and never answer the phone ever again if Rory Flynn calls.

Speaking of which...

I struggle to listen to Dad who is only a few feet away. My vision is fading in and out, but I catch the triumphant look on his face which, as usual, can't mean anything good.

"Oh, of course. That's excellent news, Rory. Thank you, my friend. I'll send someone right away."

He listens, and I catch his slight frown. His gaze meets mine, and I close my eyes, pretending to be unaware. What are they up to? And will it be dangerous for Saoirse?

"You're right, this, I should do myself. I've been waiting long enough. I'll see you there."

The renewed fear is strong enough to pierce through the cocoon created by whatever was in that wine, enough to get me in this state with just two sips. Victor stands in the corner, waiting for instructions, and I can't help the chill that's rocking my body.

I'm not naïve enough to think that I'm that much safer with Dad in the house, but he is a man with antiquated views. He might have made a promise to Victor, but it will come to pass when he says so. I don't trust Victor or his loyalty enough to believe he's willing to wait that long.

"Dad," I try. "Maybe you shouldn't go out tonight. About the wedding...There are still things we need to plan, right?"

He pats my cheek. I'm familiar with his anger which can be scary, but this is somehow worse. Did his goons find Mom? What's going to happen tonight?

"And we will, but not tonight. I think it's bedtime for you."

He nods to Victor who helps me up and toward the stairs, while I hear the door fall into the lock. It sounds cold and final.

I want to yell at him to fucking take his hands off me, but that might not be wise at this point when I can barely walk. At the door to my suite, I make myself as heavy as I possibly can, and when he has to let go for a moment, I slip inside and with a speed I didn't know I had in me, slam the door shut and lock it.

"Thank you, Victor. Good night."

"Don't lock the door, sweetheart. If you need help...Your father won't be happy."

"I'm fine, don't worry. Just one glass too many, right?"

"Aria, don't be silly. Open the door."

The barely constrained anger in his tone tells me I was right about everything. My window of opportunity is shrinking. If there ever was one.

Victor mutters an expletive.

"You can't hide from me forever," he says, but walks away, and I lean against the door, trying to stay awake while my vision is blurring. This time it's not the drugs.

I stumble into the bathroom and splash cold water on my face. In spite of the make-up I put on earlier, I look terrible. I haven't gotten much sleep except the chemically assisted one, and fear and nausea haven't helped. No wonder the Aiellos believed every word Dad told them about my "condition," or, more likely, that makes it easier for them to digest the reality of it. The sham of a marriage, the bluster, it's all too familiar to them.

Saoirse got a pretty good idea of it too, and yet she's different, her own person, her own woman. I miss her so much, and I can't help thinking that we could still be together if I hadn't messed up everything. No. It's all Dad's fault. Ironic though, that I never would have met her if I hadn't tried to get away from him and Victor.

My whole damn life, one huge irony. I allow myself some tears, because let's face it, this is pretty hopeless. I walk to the window, stumble is more like it, and look outside into the night. The view of the vast property is nice. I catch the dark outline of a guard patrolling the perimeter. No one who isn't welcomed by Antonio Bellini gets in—or out.

I have no sympathy for Victor, but in a sense, he's a prisoner too. With everything he's done for Dad, everything he knows, he won't ever get out alive. There's a difference though. He chose it, and with his choices comes a cushiony life, getting away with crimes, access to wealth, attorneys, and, if he has his way, me.

I go back to the door and put my ear against it, the wood cool against my heated face. I feel...empty. I should be more aspirational, come up with a solution. I'm smart after all, resourceful. I don't think there's anything left, but I will give it one more try. Without a plan and a vision, only an almost forgotten dream.

I open the lock, nearly stumbling to my knees in relief when Victor isn't there. It's quite true. I do need help, and I might end up in some closet and die there before anyone finds me, or one of the freaking guards will shoot me.

I assume Victor has gone to his office, biding his time. There's a light on in the living room, a glass with a clear liquid on the table, but no one's there. I shudder. If he's been drinking, it makes the most sense for me to get away from this house as soon as possible.

The front door beckons. If I could make it to the garage...No, too loud. Someone will notice right away. Past the gate, I could reach the highway and stop a car.

It's a nice fantasy, but nothing more than that, I realize as I hit the floor.

When I open my eyes, it's to the frantic voice of the woman from my dreams. Of my dreams. Semantics, because she can't be real. I almost laugh, but the sound that comes out sounds more like a cough.

"Aria. Come on, let's go."

It's a very detailed fantasy, dream, or whatever, involving all the senses. Her hair is as soft as I remember, tickling my face when she leans down. A whiff of shampoo and shower gel.

"I'm tired," I mutter.

"I know." There's a hint of relief now. "You'll be able to rest soon, I promise. Now let's get you out of here."

This isn't a dream. Saoirse is really here, she is alive and has come for me. The realization briefly overrides my rather desolate state, making me smile.

"I don't know if I can," I whisper. "If he comes back...You have to go."

She all but drags me to my feet. I can do this, hold on a little bit longer. Freedom awaits on the other side, one I've never known...I think. This time, it has to be real. I don't want to jump from train to train anymore.

"I won't leave you," she states firmly, a little out of breath, and I try to walk, make her support less of my weight, but it's hard.

"I'm sorry," I inform her. "Really sorry, but I'm happy to see you. So happy." My words are just slurred enough to let her know what's going on. Her features tense for a split second, then the reassuring smile is back in place. We are at the front door, and she opens it, somehow managing without letting me slide to the floor again, and we're outside in the cold night air. More than the water before, it helps to sober me up a little though I'm still slow, like trying to move through molasses.

"You'll be all right."

"What if Dad comes back?"

"He's in for a few surprises tonight," she says grimly, keeping her grip on me.

"Oh, good. I'm about done with his bullshit, and—"

"Shh."

Saoirse pauses to listen, then she draws me to the side and behind a mature tree.

A few seconds later, the guard walks by, rifle over his shoulder. He hasn't seen us.

There's something akin to joy bubbling up inside of me when we're past the gate. I know we're not yet safe. I can't help it. A few hours ago, I was almost ready to resign to my fate. I thought of ways to get out of this mess that were frighteningly final.

There's a reason and a purpose again.

"Thank you. Thank you so much."

The fact that she looks a little amused now tells me we're closer to making it. She's not shushing me again either.

"You're welcome. I have to admit I'm not entirely unselfish in this."

"Don't worry, Saoirse. You can be as selfish as you want once I'm sober again. The asshole put something in my wine. Can you believe it? In front of the guests."

I shake my head, a wave of vertigo hitting me, and warm strong hands steady me. Finally, there's the car.

And a sound that makes Saoirse spin around, then, a gunshot as she pushes me to the ground. I've had quite enough of this. I want to be somewhere I can stay for a while, with her, hold her close to me, but it's not going to happen anytime soon.

More shots ring out, and when she tells me to move, but stay down, I can hear it in her voice that something is wrong.

"Get inside."

I manage to drag myself into the vehicle, having a hard time not to cover my ears at the sounds of more shots. Then she's next to me, starting the car. I'm mesmerized by the wet stain on my sleeve until I realize the blood isn't mine.

We are moving, the rear window shatters into a million pieces, and for once, I do scream.

# Chapter Twenty-Seven

## Saoirse

I don't think the injury is life-threatening, but damn it, it hurts, and if I could, I'd make a U-turn and run him over for good measure. So close to a clean getaway. It wasn't my fault, or anyone's, just the fact that he's a paranoid son of a bitch. It ends tonight though, for all of them, Bellini, Orlov.

"There's a first aid kit in the glove compartment," I say. "Can you get it?"

Aria nods, a bit uncoordinated still, but obliging. She manages to get out a bandage and apply it. I grit my teeth against the pain when she presses harder on it, light-headed for a few seconds, but I put on the seatbelt and get the car moving anyway. We don't have a lot of time.

I can hear the sirens coming our way. It's not the cavalry moving in, not really, but they will certainly take care of a man shooting wildly at cars. Not that he's shooting anymore, because I left him in worse shape than I am.

I make a turn, and Aria stares at me, wide-eyed. She's more alert than when I found her, which is a good thing, because my shoulder is killing me. We might have to switch.

"Aren't we going to meet them? The police?"

Maybe the drugs have made her a little delusional too.

"No, we can't, for various reasons. They'll make a few arrests tonight though."

"You're bleeding. You need to go to a hospital!"

"I'll be okay."

There are some things that still need to stay secret, which would be hard given that hospitals are supposed to report gunshot wounds. I guess I should be grateful the bullet only grazed my arm, but it's damn painful. No such thing as "just" a flesh wound.

"This is the address we need to go. I'm not planning on passing out, but if I do, I'll need you to drive. Can you do that?"

She starts laughing but stops abruptly when she realizes I'm serious.

"I don't know. Fuck. Yes. I think I can do that."

"I wouldn't have let that happen to you," I say, and I don't have to elaborate.

Her eyes are welling up.

"I know."

I want to know how it's been going on Ryan's side, but I'm aware she can't afford to babysit either one of us right now. Willow's concerned voice floats over to me.

"You two all right? It sounded like it got pretty wild there for a moment."

I laugh wryly and then suppress a curse. Laughing makes it hurt more. "Wild is about right. Nothing we can't handle though."

Aria gives me a curious look.

"Willow," I whisper.

"Yes?"

"We'll be okay. Aria can drive, if necessary, but I think I'm going to make it."

"Good," Willow says, sounding nervous. "This was too damn close."

I don't disagree. It's not every day that I get shot at either.

"We're almost there." It's a promise, to her, to Aria, and to me, but what I'm saying to Aria between the lines, has even more meaning. I think she understands.

⁓

We are only a few miles away when I feel my fingers slip from the steering wheel for the second time. Out here, there's not a lot of traffic, but I don't want to drive into a ditch, or worse, a tree.

"Aria..."

When I first found her, she was pretty out of it, and I'm afraid to make things worse, but we can't wait here either.

"Yes. I know. Don't worry, I can make it." I park on the side of the road, and she gets out of the car and hastens to my side, then helps me outside. I can see and feel the blood seeping through the makeshift bandage she helped me attach earlier. No one has followed us all the way here, but the delay makes me uneasy. Perhaps it's the blood loss. We're lucky we didn't get pulled over, but I suppose tonight's operation requires a lot of manpower on short notice, not just from Ryan's side.

I close my eyes for a short moment, but they snap open again.

*Not yet, Saoirse.*

*Not yet.*

# Chapter Twenty-Eight

## Ruby

I still am disturbed by what I saw tonight, and that should tell me something. I've been disturbed for a while now, disappointed in the people closest to me, scared of the future. It was all well when my parents didn't care that much, and I could get away with having my nose in a book most of the time. Now I can see how it was a good thing for me to attend all those boarding schools, to go to college on the other side of the country, and study at university.

While Mom and Dad were busy with the corporation, Aunt Connie, who lives with us, arranged everything. I never understood the full scope of her advocacy for me before.

I thought life could just go on like that, that I'd find a job and live my life, show up for Thanksgiving, Christmas, and the occasional family dinner. That's not an option any longer.

My cousin Emilio was always their favorite. His parents died when he was seven and I was five. My parents took him in, mentored him, groomed him to take over the company someday.

Their hopes and mine came to an end when he was killed two months ago.

We weren't close. He was like a gruff older brother whom I barely saw or spoke to—but he's family, and I'm grieving and worried about what might come next. His killer hasn't been found. My parents are grieving too, but they also pulled me out of university to come home and discuss the next steps.

I don't want anything to do with the company and everything it stands for. I haven't told them in so many words, only Connie, hoping she might put in a good word for me...

Yet, I spent the evening at this disaster of a dinner party, with the host desperate to impress my parents, Father trying to strengthen his ties to the Russian mob, and the daughter...She was out of it. I can't prove it, but I'm pretty sure it wasn't just the wine. She didn't drink that much. Her apprehension was a stark presence in the room, only I have no idea what's really going on, and what I could do for her, other than that coffee I suggested.

Maid of honor. She didn't seem all that impressed, with me, or the idea of that wedding in general. And who can blame her? Even if I wasn't a lesbian, Victor Orlov would still be the last man on earth I'd want to marry. Yes, I know, in our circles no one really gives a damn about what we want out of life. I guess I got lucky that my family only wants me to run a business I don't care for, but make no mistake, there might be other plans down the pike. I can't think about this now, or Aria Bellini's fate. I wish I could do better, something.

Drugs, escorts, extortion and bribery, I know what's behind the curtain. People get hurt. I don't want any of it, but maybe this is my punishment for looking the other way for so long, for being relieved as long as Emilio was going to take the reins, and I could live anywhere I wanted to, in blissful ignorance.

But maybe there is another way.

The thought forms in mind, taking shape as I sit at breakfast with my parents, half-listening when they instruct me on yet another dinner coming up, my slow introduction to the community. No one needed to see much of a nerdy bookworm when brilliant enigmatic Emilio was on the job. Now they only have me left, and I know they're worried.

I almost laugh, but I don't want to tip them off. It's all so ridiculous. This family, the luxury we live in, was all built on crime, someone else's blood. More people are going to die, and they are worried about me wearing the right shoes and make-up for the occasion?

I force myself to pay more attention when the subject shifts to the Bellinis. There was some sort of raid last night after we left, and...

They are angry, but I barely suppress the smile.

There is another way. There has got to be.

# Chapter Twenty-Nine

## Aria

Saoirse is still standing, but ghostly pale by the time we make it to the front door. Once I take in the surroundings, it's not a surprise any longer to see Rory Flynn open the door, a woman his age behind him who immediately starts fussing over her.

"Frankly, you look terrible, love. The doctor is here, she'll take care of you. Come with me."

I want to go, too, instead I'm left standing in a more than awkward silence with Flynn. He probably feels the same about me, not that I have it in me to have sympathy for him. If he hadn't teamed up with Dad…

Then again, I know that my father would have simply found someone else to lure into this undertaking, and things might have been much worse. I shudder, thinking of how narrowly we escaped, my stomach still doing flip-flops as I am drawn down the rabbit hole. Saoirse could have been killed. I could have been…

"You want something to drink?"

I shake myself out of the horror. We are here. Saoirse is getting help, and my mind is getting clearer by the minute.

"Water maybe? Thanks."

When he's gone, I don't wait but walk into the direction where Saoirse went with the older woman. I open a door, then another, until I find the right one. There's indeed a woman in a white coat disinfecting the wound before she applies a fresh bandage. She doesn't look up, but I can sense the tension. She's not happy to be here either, but from the looks of it, she's doing her job well.

"We're almost done here." Saoirse's attempt at a reassuring smile falls a little flat, as I can see the lines of pain in her face. It's reassuring nonetheless that a real doctor—I hope—is tending to her. I step closer and take her hand. I want to ask so many questions, but it's all still too muddled, and I assume that no one will come after us here. If anyone tries, I trust that someone like Flynn has adequate security as well. I am so tired.

"Doc, I want you to look at her too, maybe take some blood. She was drugged."

"Yes, Ma'am."

I'm not sure if there's a hint of sarcasm to her tone. I might have been mistaken, because after she finishes up with Saoirse, she pulls off her gloves, washes her hands and puts on a new set.

"Sit, please." She arranges everything she needs on a side table, and a moment later I feel the sting of the needle, flinching. "This will only take a second."

I can't help it, panic coursing through my body at the reminder, but Saoirse's gaze at me, warm and understanding, anchors me in the present. The doctor fills a vial and removes the tourniquet around my arm.

"I'll get this tested ASAP," she says to Saoirse, who nods. "Any other exams we need to do? I understand you were subjected to—"

"No," I say quickly. "No, I'm fine otherwise. Thank you."

Saoirse's relief is palpable, or perhaps it's mine I'm projecting.

"I need to have a word with Rory," she says. "Do you think you could hold on a few more minutes? Then I swear, I'll find us somewhere to sleep."

"Here?"

Of course, here. I don't think either one of us can go on much longer, and it looks like we are safe, but I have a hard time getting past the fact that Flynn was the one who sold me out in the first place.

"I know what you're thinking," Saoirse whispers to me as we walk back to the living room, the doctor's heels clicking on the hardwood floor. She seems eager to leave. "It will be okay. This time, for real. Your father is in one hell of a lot of trouble."

It's...good news. I'm not sure if I can believe it, not yet. It's unreal, all of it, so I have to cling to the only thing that feels right, her presence, her hand in mine.

"Victor—"

Her face hardens for a brief moment, and she squeezes my hand gently.

"You won't have to worry about him anymore."

"He's gone?"

"He is."

She says this with such certainty, I don't ask her any more questions after that. There's no regret and no remorse over this outcome. We sit in the living room where Rory hands me a glass of water, his expression unreadable. His wife, Ciara, is present too, and they talk to Saoirse in hushed tones, giving me curious looks every once in a while. There's regret in their expressions too, and I can only imagine, but it gives me hope.

Maybe they do understand where they went wrong. It's all relative in this context, but I take what I can get.

"We'll take it one step at a time," Flynn says. "You're welcome as long as you'd like to stay. Both of you," he adds.

Despite being exhausted, I can't help being curious, as there's obviously history between the people in this room.

"We appreciate it," Saoirse says. "But we'll look for something tomorrow. Stay under the radar until we can figure out the next steps. Thank you."

"It's not a problem." He casts a look at me, then back to her. "You know, the reason we knew that Tommy had left you the cottage was that this was always the plan. No strings attached. And I swear to you, no one knows about it except us—and you two, of course."

That is new information, but I trust that I'll hear more about it after we get some sleep.

"That's good to know, because I'd like to go back there sometime."

The quick glance she gives me is hopeful, and I feel the happy warmth battling the residual fear and pain into submission. There is a life for us beyond all this.

"Now, I think we could all use a drink. I got some of our finest from the cellar once I knew you were on the way."

I swear Saoirse is about to roll her eyes, but she doesn't protest.

_ele_

I'm certainly not a connoisseur of fine whiskey, but even I can tell that it's an excellent product. Ciara offers dark chocolates along with it, and the ever-present feeling of dread recedes some more, as I understand our present situation much better. Sometimes it's worth it to find allyship with the lesser evil. These people aren't innocent, but neither are we. All of us need to find a way to move forward somehow.

I have no regrets any longer, about where we are, about that whiskey, when we lie together in the queen bed in the guestroom not much later, and I cradle her, mindful of her injury. That damn flight on the private plane, the constant threat of what would happen once the wedding was a done deal, it all seems far away now.

I am still amazed that someone would go to those lengths for me, the way she did. That bullet, I know, was for me, because he knew I'd never be the obedient wife that Dad had promised him.

Saoirse kept all her promises and then some.

"I'm sorry," I whisper. "I'm so sorry. I should have believed you. I...I didn't know what to think."

She turns to me, winces, but reaches out to put a finger on my lips.

"Stop. I should have explained about the money, and Rory's involvement in this. People have lied to you your entire life. I get it."

That's probably letting me off the hook easily. I appreciate it. There's no further I can go tonight, nothing else I can do but to carefully lean into her.

"Thank you."

She reaches out to brush her finger over my cheek. I've never felt this cherished, seen this much. It's an unfamiliar, amazing feeling.

"There will be time to clear up everything," she promised.

I'll be around for every moment of it. And maybe, along the way, our shared dream can come true.

# Chapter Thirty

## Saoirse

We will leave as soon as we can, but for now, with the painkillers working, I'm happy to stay a little while longer in the warmth of Aria's embrace, in one of Rory's guest suites of all places. I have to give it to him, he's come a long way from the days of raised eyebrows over his grandson's princess obsession, or his daughter-in-law's bisexuality.

Not that anything happened in this room other than sleep, and it wouldn't have even if Orlov hadn't taken a shot at me. Not because of Rory's possible sensibilities, but because of the fact that the past few days have been exhausting. We both needed sleep, in an environment where we could let down our guards for a few hours.

I'm not fooling myself into thinking it will last forever. Farmer will do what she can, but leaving a dead body for the team moving in wasn't planned. I still don't have any regrets, shudder at the thought of what Aria's fate could have been. I'll admit to wanting to protect her to the point of compulsion. Maybe it's a bit over the line. He wanted to own her, and it's not a secret what that would have meant. It's never going to happen now.

I'm quite sure Aria and I will both have to answer questions eventually.

And there's another touchy subject I haven't been able to address with Aria yet. I cast a glance at my phone and decide it can wait until after breakfast.

I wonder if much has changed in this household—yesterday, it didn't look like it, but I'm fairly sure striking a compromise with the FBI meant that Rory had to give up some familiar comforts, maybe had some assets frozen.

I reluctantly leave the bed to wash up and get dressed, and I open the door. I can hear the sounds of dishes and cutlery, and the smells of food and coffee wafting up to us. With a smile, I shake my head. If anything, Rory has not cut down on staff.

"You're up."

Aria is, too, looking adorable in the casual nightshirt, her hair slightly disheveled, her gaze telling me she's not quite awake yet. New clothes were laid out for us last night. All around service.

"You can take your time getting ready. They're preparing breakfast downstairs."

She nods, and it occurs to me that she's not new to this.

"I'll just take a quick shower. I could really use some caffeine."

I wait until she's ready, text Willow and thank her meanwhile. No news from Special Agent Ryan Farmer is probably good news. We are going to get through this. Even though a dose of painkillers is imminent. I think back to that moment, returning fire, watching him drop to the ground, with grim satisfaction.

*Look who's still standing.*

~·~

"Wow, I can't believe how hungry I am," Aria exclaims when she comes out of the bathroom, fully dressed. "You're ready?"

"Wait," I say gently, touching her shoulder when she's about to open the door to go downstairs.

I got another text from Willow which prompts me not to delay this important conversation any further. There will be another guest who can likely fill in some blanks, but I don't want Aria to think I kept yet another secret from her.

"What is it? Are you in pain?"

"No, I'm good," I say, hoping my face matches my words. "It's about...Bellini."

"I hope he's going to prison for a long time. Anything I can do to make that happen."

"I know. There's something else that Willow found out, and we can do more research together if you like. I'll help you any way I can."

"Saoirse, you're scaring me." There's a hint of impatience in her tone now.

"I'm sorry about that. Look, it would appear that Bellini is not your biological father."

"What?" Her face is blank for a few seconds, and I'm not sure she heard me correctly. When Aria speaks, the meaning is crystal clear though. "I mean, that's a relief. I'm glad not to be associated with him in that way. And it makes a lot of sense now, how we never really had a connection."

I could tell her that the sort of connection she's talking about isn't always a given with biological parents, but now's not the time when she still has so many questions.

"But how—?" she starts, then stops again.

"Willow found Beatrice and got in touch with her, and...apparently your mother was pressured into marrying Bellini when her parents found out she was pregnant."

Aria blinks. I'm sorry for having to spring all of it on her now, but we only have a small window.

"Did Willow find out who he is? My biological father?"

"She didn't say. Maybe she doesn't know yet. But Aria, she's here."

"Who, Willow?"

"Your mother."

For a few moments, she has that terrified, deer-in-the-head-lights look on her face that makes me want to scoop her up and take her away to a secret place. Not that I could physically do it at the moment. Probably, in a life-or-death situation, but we've had enough of those.

The next part isn't going to be dangerous. It's going to be emotional.

Aria straightens, and her voice is firm when she speaks.

"All right. Let's go meet her then. We might as well get all the answers today."

I pull her to me, and she rests her forehead against mine. We stay like that for a few seconds, until we can no longer put off the inevitable.

When we come down to the dining room where breakfast is being served, Marina Bellini, née Cacciatore, sits at the table with Rory and Ciara.

Aria stiffens for a few long, painful seconds before she takes a deep breath.

"Mom?"

I'm not sure what I'm expecting. We imagined from the start that Marina would have a lot of answers for us. Mostly, I wanted this for Aria, but I can tell it's not going to be easy.

"Aria." She gets to her feet, hesitantly steps closer. "I thought I'd never see you again."

Ciara smiles widely, while Rory is focusing on the plate in front of him. It does smell good enough for my stomach to rumble, but I'm watching the two women closely.

"I kind of thought the same thing," Aria admits, and they hug, though it's brief and a tad awkward. I'm sad for them, the lost time.

My own family was very different, nothing much to repair. My father was emotionally abusive and spent most of what he earned on alcohol and gambling, my mother too tired to care about anything or anyone. What's done is done, and in a way, it's true for Aria and Marina as well.

Even if what we've hoped for comes true and neither of them needs to hide anymore, that time is gone.

"Sit and eat, please," Rory urges. "It's going to be a long day. Saoirse, I need to talk to you later. We're going to give the authorities everything they need to take out Bellini, but there needs to be some containment."

Marina laughs mirthlessly. "For you. No one is completely altruistic in anything, I assume. But I swear, I'm going to do my part. I'm done hiding."

Aria gives her a reluctant smile.

I hope they are going to be okay, but I don't know just yet.

And I'll have to remind Rory that while I'm grateful for his assistance in this case, I'll never work for him again.

---

Ryan arrives not long after we've finished breakfast, one of her colleagues with her. She's tight-lipped, not revealing much, but she spends almost two hours behind closed doors with Marina while the colleague talks to Rory.

I wonder, would he mind if I got into that whiskey some more? I admit I'll miss getting this particular brand for free. But that's not the most important thing right now. I reach out to touch Aria's shoulder, startling her out of her reverie.

"You got to speak a bit with your mom earlier."

"Yes. I can't thank you enough for everything you've done for me. I honestly had given up on ever seeing her again, and..." She swallows. "I think I would have been okay with it if she was safe. But this, it's going to be hard, but it's important. For all of us to be safe. As Rory said, the dominoes will fall, and I guess that'll be good for him."

"He's got to take it easy too if he wants the FBI at a distance," I say, aware that her words don't reveal all that much. I know that she has no trouble with whatever is necessary to put the man who nearly sold her, in prison—even if he was her father.

"Sure. As for Mom...She wants to keep in touch."

"That's a good thing."

"It is." She smiles but can't quite keep back the tears. "I don't know what I was thinking. She left, because she had no choice, and then there was no way she could come back. I get that. She didn't have a Willow or an FBI agent on her side. Or an Irish mob boss," she says with a snort.

I feign indignation. "You might not want to say that out loud in this house."

We both laugh, which hurts, but it's definitely better than crying.

"I'll remember that," she says dryly. "My point is, once this is over, things are likely not going to go the way I fantasized. Then again...In Paris, I had a dream about a gorgeous red-headed woman. And she turned out to be real."

I can't help smiling at her choice words. After the recent run-ins with one Victor Orlov, I know I still look worse for wear.

"That's very generous of you to say. And dreams have significance." My grandmother used to claim that, and perhaps there was a point to her superstition. "You'll do what you need to do," I add. "Did you learn anything else about your father?" I ask.

"I did." Her eyes mist over. "I can't believe my grandparents did that to Mom, forcing her to marry when...He died. In Afghanistan."

"I'm so sorry." I embrace her gently, and she leans into me, her exhaustion matching mine.

"Thank you," she whispers. "She's going to send me some pictures. I wish I could have met him. But I want to make sure I don't waste any more time with her. I'm just not sure...where to start."

"That's understandable. It's been a lot. I think your mother is aware that you both need to come to terms with the past. She might like to come visit us."

"At the cottage?" Aria asks, her eyes widening as she's reading my mind. "You still want me there?"

My expression must have been enough, because she leans in to kiss me, holding me so tightly I can't help the sounds of pain.

"I love you, but...ouch."

Ryan Farmer and her colleague, who have entered the room, give us quizzical looks while we hurry to straighten our clothes.

They are ready for us.

We might as well get this over with now.

# Chapter Thirty-One

## Aria

There is no time to get our stories straight, but I guess Saoirse or Rory would have told me if there was a need. I focus on the most important points—I had no specific knowledge of Antonio Bellini's criminal acts until I realized that my mother wasn't just missing, she had escaped. I didn't seek out the authorities because at that time, I was on the run as well.

Farmer records diligently as I describe my mad dash across several cities.

"At first it was only a feeling that someone might be following me, but when they tried to drag me into the car, Saoirse saved me. We...went to different places, friends of hers, hotels."

The corner of her mouth lifts into a wry smile. I'm not sure how aware she is of Saoirse's friends and the safehouses.

"Anyway, in the hotel in Hamburg, they caught up with us. Victor hit Saoirse, and they took me. They..." The air in the room seems to be getting thinner. I can feel the color drain from my face as I describe the situation. "He threatened to hurt her, or innocent bystanders if I didn't go with them. He made me get into a waiting car, and my father..." Old habits die hard, I guess. "Bellini was there. We went to the airport and took a chartered private plane from there." I sit up straighter. "Wait! We never went through security, because he had some connections with a local politician. Did you find out who that was?"

"Interpol did, yes," she said wryly. "He's one of the reasons why Mr. Bellini won't make bail. Let's circle back to Mr. Orlov for a moment. Did you see him get shot?"

"No," I admit. "But we were running for our lives. He kept shooting. Saoirse kept us both alive."

"And we appreciate that outcome," she says, continuing to take notes.

"Appreciate? Do you have any idea what would have happened if that wedding had actually taken place?"

She looks chastised, haunted even, for a moment.

"We don't condone vigilante acts, Ms. Bellini, but I'm glad you're here to tell the story."

"Is that all?"

"Tell me a bit more about those dinner guests, Mr. and Mrs. Aiello."

That is a surprise.

"I'm vaguely aware of them. I saw their names a few times on company papers, and I've met them before. But last night...You know I was drugged. It's all foggy. I was out on the floor when Saoirse found me."

Again, that haunted gaze.

"Have you been to a hospital?"

"She has received excellent private care. And Saoirse did what she had to do. I'd always vouch for her character."

Rory Flynn has entered the room, and his unsolicited contribution to this conversation is almost...comical. Agent Farmer and I exchange a look, and I could swear there was some shared amusement, since we both know what Saoirse would think of this compliment.

At the thought, I'm overcome by a wave of longing. I need to be with her. Now.

It's never been so clear to me that the only time I felt truly at home was with her.

"Thank you, Mr. Flynn," I say. "She'll appreciate you saying that." And to Farmer: "When do you think we can leave the country?"

She's back to her reserved, cranky self.

"Not in the next few days, I wouldn't recommend it. I'll let you know."

I don't wait any longer, but head for the door and yank it open, almost making Saoirse tumble into the room. Farmer is shaking her head.

Laughter is tickling my throat. Will this roller coaster of emotions ever end?

"Were you listening in?" I ask. "I swear I didn't give her any salacious details."

She sort of rolls her eyes at me and then draws me to her, kissing me far too passionately for the audience. Not that I care, even when I hear someone clear their throat.

# Chapter Thirty-Two

## Saoirse

Time to pack our bags once more. It seems unreal, yet it hasn't been a month since I was first back in Ireland, minding my own business and exploring my ancestry. This might become more important than I ever imagined. I have an idea that might work out for us in the long run...If Aria still wants that, of course. The long run.

It's strange to think that for most of my life, I didn't think that love was in the cards. Not in the way so many people dream of, and, if I was honest, maybe I did too. A time or two, I did ponder what might have happened if Tommy had never met Courtney. Would things have ended the same, that night in the alley? It's impossible to say now.

When I first traveled to Ireland, I had the idea of selling the cottage as soon as possible, getting rid of every connection with the Flynn family. I had given them enough, hadn't I? This wasn't my home, but another complication I had to deal with.

The longer I stayed, the more I started enjoying the surroundings, the people who started to greet me on the street, the hospitality of Keira at the pub, and others.

Before the idea could fully form, I got that call which led me to Aria. Aria who had been searching for home as well, after trying to get away from another powerful family.

Well, perhaps not so powerful anymore. Aria's grandparents were clearly in the wrong making her daughter marry Bellini, the kind of fate that Aria only narrowly escaped—but they did insist on iron-clad contracts, and the moment Marina found out, her life was in danger.

Whatever assets of Bellini that will not be seized in an extensive investigation into multiple crimes, including attempted kidnapping and murder beyond those past days, will go to her, and eventually Aria.

No wonder he was so intent on finding her. The authorities might even look into the deaths of Marina's parents.

"What are you thinking?" Aria asks, looking up from her book she's now close to finishing. We have moved to yet another hotel, this time, laying low for real. I'm getting a bit antsy, but she keeps telling me I'm recovering from injury. It's true that I am, but that doesn't mean I'm not ready for more than cuddling.

"Things we could do before dinner."

She smiles widely. "I thought you were tired."

"No. I just wanted to lure you into bed with me."

That, and my hopes about what the future could look like, are becoming clearer, but there's time to tackle all of that.

"You're lucky you can lure me just about anywhere." She lays the book on the nightstand and turns to me. "I know what's on your mind, and believe me, I'm more than willing, but maybe we should wait a little longer. You are—"

"Still recovering, I know. I wasn't thinking acrobatics either."

Aria laughs at my matter-of-fact delivery, her hand on my hip moving lower slowly.

"You do have a point. If you stay still, this might work." Her fingers tease beneath the waistband of my shorts, and I draw a sharp breath.

"Oh, I think it will."

She scoots a bit closer, carefully, and my body and mind race down a one-way-street when she touches me. I can't hold in the moan to save my life.

Her movements are slow and torturous, her kisses soft.

"I see you've given this some thought."

Right now, it's all I can think about, Aria, this beautiful woman handling my body with such care and passion. Right, I have to be careful, stay still, not pull anything but...Nothing matters but to let it all go, let go in her arms, because it's a space where I, too, can be safe.

"Come with me to Ireland. When this is all over, we can build a life there."

It might be the mind-shattering orgasm that has loosened my tongue, it might be much too early to bring this up, but Aria doesn't seem to mind.

"I can't wait," she whispers and starts kissing her way down my body.

# Chapter Thirty-Three

## Aria

The past few weeks have been taxing, though compared to everything we've been through already, it's all relative. Saoirse has been healing, sometimes frustrated through the process, and we've found ways to deal with that. Just reminiscing gives me that warm, tingly feeling, inappropriate as I visit the company with my lawyer, sorting out the details of my future involvement in it, if any.

I quit my job. The company is and will be under investigation for the foreseeable future, and a few other arrests have already been made, men in higher positions loyal to my father who made sure that he could present a clean front, a mirage given the beast lurking beneath.

I have decided I don't want anything to do with it. If at the end of that very long tunnel, there's still some money left for Mom, and me, I'll put it to good use, hopefully offset some of the hurt that's been done.

As for me—I have a degree and still, a now smaller amount of money stashed away.

Tonight, I'm using a tiny part of it to take Saoirse to dinner. My...girlfriend? It's hard to pin down. The woman I can't keep my hands off, who has risked her life to save mine more than once. I haven't done much to pay her back...which doesn't include the amazing things she can do to my body, especially now that she has her full flexibility back.

Tonight marks yet another a milestone.

Farmer told us we were free to go, and now, there's a lot to discuss. I think. I know Saoirse has been pondering her future, possible career moves, as well. We can't stay in the hotel forever. It's been comfortable. I'm a bit nervous as the hostess leads us to our table, and we order champagne from the young server who comes to see us.

It brings me back to that wild night when we drank whiskey in Rory Flynn's living room. All those connections, much as we try, they will never go away completely. What Bellini and my mother did, one for his ego, the other one for survival, both leaving me behind in a way. Saoirse's parents, the Flynns, Tommy.

I'd like to believe that we found something that supersedes all of those connections. I just need to know that she feels the same.

"So, here we are." My voice sounds a bit off, and I clear my throat. She smiles gently.

"We are. Everything is cleared up at the company now?"

"On my side, yes. I won't even pretend to know everything illegal that was going on just yet, and I seriously doubt that much will be left when the FBI is through with it."

"Yeah. I'm sorry."

"Don't be. That was never mine to begin with...Or his. Anyway. You still want to work in your job after all? Freelance maybe?"

"That's what I was trying to decide back in Ireland," she says. "Obviously I'm still drawn to it. But mostly I was...am drawn to you."

That is encouraging.

"I'm happy to hear that."

Which means...

"It might sound crazy, but I'd love to go back soon, and...I meant it. I'd love for you to come with me. If you want."

"Yes, yes I do," I say so fast it sounds like one word, and I blush, because of my eagerness, and the realization of what phrase I used.

The server brings our wine and appetizer plates. We thank them, smile, Saoirse tasting the first sip and giving her okay. A few seconds pass in silence, before she says,

"You know, I didn't mean just as a vacation. Am I being ridiculous?"

The instant joy at her confession leaves me breathless for a moment. Speechless, too, because I catch her worried gaze.

"No. I mean, no, that's not ridiculous at all. I was hoping you'd want that."

She looks a little wistful at that.

"I've been wanting this for a while now. It seems selfish, since you have so much to figure out, and your mom is here...but I couldn't help it."

"I want to be there, with you. What's left here..." It's my turn to go for the more somber subject. "I'm so grateful she's alive and won't have to run any longer, and we'll definitely keep in touch. But I don't think our relationship can ever be the same, or what I once hoped for. I don't blame her. I need to make decisions for my own life."

"I have some ideas." Saoirse sits up straighter, and now digs into her appetizer with gusto. Perhaps she, too, has been waiting for a sign. We are better than we were, but I guess we could still improve our communication skills.

"I love it. I love you."

She reaches out to take my hand. "I love you too, Aria. And I know it's not going to be easy, but I looked into some of our options. I could get dual citizenship. That would help in the long run, and..."

I hold my breath. Is my nightmare going to become a fairytale?

"We'll figure it out, I promise," Saoirse says. "If you don't love it, we can always come back. We will have to a few times, anyway, but if you can imagine it, I'll do whatever it takes to make it home for you."

I'm not disappointed, on the contrary. I don't need a contract to confirm what I know.

"Home is wherever you are," I say.

—ell—

A week later, we are in paradise, or at least it feels like that to me. Hikes along the cliffs with breathtaking views, long evenings at the pub where Keira is clearly rooting for our happy ending, because she finds ways to make our table extra romantic. Saoirse is this close to rolling her eyes, but she loves it just as much.

She is looking into her options for starting her own business here once all the immigration paperwork is completed and approved, or perhaps freelancing for a friend. Keira tells me I could always come work at the pub to get started, and I might take her up on that offer once I have a work permit.

It didn't take me long to take a liking to the people in this town, as everyone has welcomed us. Some, like Keira, are genuinely excited about our plans.

Meanwhile we are staying at the place I thought of as home the moment we walked through the door.

It's furnished and decorated tastefully, and I can see some of Saoirse's touches from when she first came here. A bit strange to think we sleep in the same bed her former employee's son and his wife did when they first met, but that's beside the point.

I mention it to Saoirse when we sit in the living room late at night. We're long over the jet lag, but there's still a lot to talk about, to sort it. I'm grateful that Saoirse's eyes are no longer tinged with sadness when she talks about Tommy Flynn.

"If that's too weird for you, we can always change it."

"It's fine for now," I assure her. "Many more people slept—and did more—in the hotel rooms we stayed in." I have to laugh when she makes a face.

"All right, I get your point. Since we didn't have dessert earlier..."

"You are insatiable, but I love it."

She's cracking up now. "Thank you, and I am, but I meant an actual nightcap with something sweet if you're up for it."

"I am." The yawn comes out of nowhere.

"Don't worry, I'll go get it."

I lean back against the couch, the dancing flames in the fire-place almost hypnotic. It's cooler here than I'm used to, but also cozy, and I'm head over heels, so I don't mind at all. The recent past, constant fears that were vague at first, and became very specific once I dared to rebel, feel blessedly distant, and not just because of the geographical distance. I love it here, to share this with Saoirse. Comforted by those thoughts, I am nearly asleep when she returns with a tray holding two glasses of whiskey—from Flynn's send-off gift—chocolates and a small velvet-covered box. I sit up straight, my fatigue instantly forgotten.

"Since we're making plans for the future..." She holds my gaze, and I am more enthralled than ever. She led us through fire, and we came out alive on the other side. It's her courage that gave me mine, to work with the authorities best I could to help end Dad's reign. It's because of her that I realized it was worth leaving my fears behind. My eyes are welling up, and I can't even be sure—

Okay. When she opens the box and holds it out to me, I now can be sure. The white gold ring with the simple diamond is elegant and beautiful. I can't hold back the gasp.

"It will be a long wait and a mountain of paperwork either way, but I can't think of anything I want more than to start over, here, with you by my side. For a long time, I didn't think I even deserved this. You have changed my life, Aria. And I'm afraid I have no long eloquent speech prepared, but I do love you. More than I ever thought I could love anyone. Will you marry me?"

"Yes." This time, I don't hesitate. "I want to. I will." I hug her close, we kiss, and then she puts the ring on my finger.

It's been a hard-earned victory, but we've made it.

This is the peace we deserve.

# Epilogue

## Ruby

I have memorized the address, destroyed all evidence that I ever looked it up. No one knows, no one suspects anything, and it will have to stay that way for a while to come. Weeks. Months maybe.

The headlines I see about the Bellinis don't surprise me at all. Father is furious, conferring with his associates almost daily. Businessmen, influential people in politics and law enforcement. They need to lay low, he says, in case Bellini gets stupid ideas.

I don't know what Aria did or said that started this avalanche, or maybe it wasn't her at all, but all of it confirms what I've been wrestling with for a long time now. Only, it will be this much harder, because I have no one on my side.

For me, for the life that might be possible someday, I have to try.

# Saoirse

*A year later*

W hen I unlock the front door, a delicious smell wafts over to me from the kitchen, and even though I'm bone-tired, I can't help smiling. I am beyond fortunate. Dual citizenship makes my life a lot easier, and by proxy, that of my wife. We still need to be patient regarding Aria's paperwork, because mine came first, then the wedding, but we are optimistic.

Bellini's arrest had a ripple effect, even internationally, and the life we have now...I try not to be superstitious about it, instead believe that it's the life we deserve.

I found a few freelance jobs, the latest, providing security for a local businesswoman. My knowledge has been helpful coordinating with law enforcement, and given my past, that's almost funny. We abide by the law, but there's nothing straight or narrow about it.

Aria has stayed in touch with her mother, who came to the wedding as well.

And being in love with her as I am, in over my head, truly, madly, deeply, past grievances don't cut so painfully any longer.

I said goodbye to Rory and Ciara knowing it was the end of an era.

This is my era of peace.

I walk into the kitchen, and Aria turns to me with a smile. The wonderful smell stems from the cookies that are fresh out of the oven, and she's made tea. A fire is crackling in the fireplace in the living room.

"Welcome home," she says, and opens her arms.

It truly is.

# About the Author

B arbara Winkes writes sapphic crime drama and Christ-mas romance. She loves writing characters who get the job done, whether it's stopping a predator or saving cherished traditions—while still making time for love. She lives with her wife in Quebec City.

barbarawinkes.com

# Acknowledgments

T hank you –

Dominique, as always!

Persephone Black for sharing my books with more fans of sapphic Mafia romance, and my readers for believing in this universe where women color outside the lines.

# Also By Barbara Winkes

**The Crossing Lines Trilogy**
*Undercover*
*Redemption*
*Vengeance*

**The Connected Series**
*Promised to the Queen*
*Drawn to the Enemy*
*Tempted by the Protector*